NOT THE DUKE YOU MARRY

THE KENT'S ROW DUCHESSES
BOOK THREE

JESS MICHAELS

For Jen Myers, who made the best friend-neighbor a reality for me. Miss you so much now that we've moved but I know you're always right there no matter how far apart we are.

And to Michael. Where would I be without you? I can't even picture it. Love you so, so much.

PROLOGUE

July 1802

Theodore Tinsley would one day be the Duke of Lightmorrow. That was knowledge that had been all but beaten into him from the earliest moment he could recall. It was also the fact about himself that he detested most. If he had been the son of someone else, if there had been less expectation placed on his future, perhaps his father wouldn't have hated him so much.

And the current duke did seem to *hate* him. Theo's entire growing up, his father had been harsh and cold, cruel and baiting. And now it was his eighteenth birthday and Theo shuddered to think what would happen. After all, he'd started the day in a most unpleasant exchange with the duke and one of his father's closest friends, the Earl of Etheridge. An argument that had reached its peak nearly with blows.

And now his father had some cronies over and he had insisted that Theo join them for drinks. Since Etheridge was one of them, Theo couldn't imagine the night was going to be pleasant.

He walked down the long hallway toward the parlor where his father and his friends were gathered. He could hear them as he approached—it seemed they had not waited for him to begin the drinking. He smoothed his jacket and wished he hadn't run his hand through his hair after he left his chamber, but it would have to do.

He was about to push the door open when he heard his father say, "—turning down such a fine opportunity. He's a waste."

"Oh, don't be so hard on the boy," he heard another voice say, and then a pause. "After all, this generation is a disappointment in general, it isn't only your son."

Theo froze, hand outstretched as he realized they were discussing *him*. That his father was talking about him in these terms in front of these men. And now they were laughing as the duke launched into a story from five years ago when Theo had wept over the death of a barn cat he'd adored. As his father gave the details with scorn dripping from every word, Theo was yanked back in time to his father's rage over his emotional display. Apparently the duke had squirreled away these facts to bring out to humiliate him.

And Theo was supposed to drink with these men? How could he? How could he do that when all he wanted to do was burst into that room and tell his father to go to hell?

He drew in a shallow breath at that thought. There would be consequences to such a thing. While it was fine for the duke to humiliate *him* in front of guests, Theo knew from experience that the punishment if he did the same would be swift. Occasionally violent. But perhaps it was worth it.

He pushed his shoulders back and leaned forward, ready to burst in when he felt a hand close around the inside of his elbow. He looked down to see Lady Bernadette, the daughter of the very man he'd had such an ugly exchange with, Etheridge. She was clinging to him, gazing up at him with wide brown eyes.

He started because he'd been thinking a great deal about her lately.

He had known Bernadette for years, though he'd once heard someone call her Etta and he'd never thought of her as anything else since. Because their fathers were friends, she had long been a fixture at gatherings. Despite the fact she was three years younger than Theo, he had never minded when she joined with any of the gangs of children to run through the woods or fish or skip rocks.

She was sharp-witted and kind to others. She always seemed aware of anyone who was on the outside looking in and she made people feel welcome. *He* felt welcome when he was with her, and that was an uncommon enough emotion in his not-particularly-long life.

In the last year or so, he had also noticed that she was becoming very pretty. She looked *extremely* pretty as she held firm to him, her soft eyes kind and steady on his. Calming.

He needed calming during this party, especially, thanks to that unpleasant encounter he'd had with both his father and hers that morning over her. It had clearly been the reason his father had begun talking about him in such a disparaging tone now. He pushed those thoughts away.

"Don't," she said softly.

Theo swallowed hard, feeling the heat fill his cheeks as he realized she had heard exactly what had been said about him and that long ago pain. He shook free of her. "What do you know about it?" he whispered, so the men inside wouldn't hear them.

"I know that if you go in there you'll only provide them with more entertainment," she replied gently. "Please, Theo, don't do it. Come with me instead."

He stared at the door. "He's…he's expecting me."

She shrugged. "So?"

He pursed his lips. There would be consequences for not making an appearance, too. But right now the idea of marching off with this girl was just as bewitching as crashing into the room and calling his father out for his horrible behavior.

"Fine," Theo ground out, and followed as Etta slipped down the hall and into a little used room that led to the terrace overlooking the garden. He didn't seem capable of doing anything *but* following her when she went down the stairs and through the garden paths to a gazebo on the edge of the property.

She smiled at him as she entered and walked over to look out over the rolling hills down to the lake half a mile away. "How many times did we all play games out there?" she asked.

He shook his head. "Too many to count."

She glanced at him. "I'm sorry about what he said, Theo," she said softly. "That he made sport of your pain and loss."

He forced his usual grin, his mask. "Don't worry about it."

"He shouldn't have done it," she continued anyway. "But then again, he's always been a cruel person."

Theo jerked his head toward her. No one had ever dared to make that fact plain to him. And yet this girl did it so easily. Like she understood it. And perhaps she did. Her own father and mother were as cold as Theo's.

"I suppose he wants to make me tough," he said, repeating the line his father had always said.

She shook her head. "They *always* claim that. But I wonder what would have happened if any of them had tried to make us safe. Or happy. Or comfortable."

Theo shifted under that statement, trying not to picture it because it hurt too much. When he didn't speak, she edged a little closer. "Happy birthday."

"You know it's my birthday?" he asked.

She nodded. "My maid told me. One of your servants must have mentioned it below stairs. How old are you?"

"Eighteen," he said, and shook his head. "I suppose he'll grant me one of his lesser titles now. And I'll be even further under his thumb."

"But not forever," she said with a wobbly smile. "One day you'll be free, Theo. You'll get to do whatever you want without him having any say." She turned away and looked off into the distance again. "It won't be that way for me."

"What are they trying to trap you into doing?" he asked, though he already knew.

"They're already working to marry me off," Etta said. "Interviewing candidates like it's a vocation." She twisted her face. "I'm sure it will all be arranged by the time I'm sixteen and then there will be no future at all to dream of."

Theo bent his head. Yes, there it was. The marriage. It was one his father had tried to arrange for *him* not twelve hours before. She obviously had no idea of that fact. Or that he had refused the match loudly and strenuously because he couldn't bear his father and the earl's manipulation. Their assumptions that he would come in line. His control had been stretched as they made their plans and he'd lashed out and made it clear he wouldn't be forced.

But even if that hadn't happened, he never would have considered marriage because he was *eighteen*. He didn't want to have his life laid out in front of him. As Etta had said, soon enough he would have some freedom from what his father wanted. The last thing he needed to do was be leg shackled.

And yet, for a brief moment, Theo could see the clearest picture of himself standing beside this girl. Of them walking off into the sunset that was starting off in the distance. Of them leaving their overbearing families behind and making some kind of new life together.

He blinked as that idea overwhelmed him. No. He was just feeling vulnerable and had been comforted by her. That rare experience made him confused, nothing more.

He stepped back from her a fraction. "I really should go in. He'll rage even more if I don't."

Her gaze held his but a moment more and then it dropped away. "Of course. I'm sure I'll see you later for supper."

He inclined his head and started toward the house, but then he turned back. "Etta?" he said.

She started at the use of her nickname and pivoted to face him. "Y-yes?"

"Thank you," he said, mustering all the sincerity he usually shunned in favor of the shield of humor. "What you did was...it was kind. And I hope whoever your parents match you with, that he'll appreciate that."

For a moment he saw her gaze flit over him with longing. But then the expression was gone. She smiled and was serene, like she'd made peace with whatever would come next. "Thank you, Theo."

He left her to return to his father, and pushed away any feelings that standing next to her had stirred up. He had a great deal else to manage at the moment. He would just need to forget the girl in the gazebo, forget the vulnerability he'd felt comfortable to share.

Forget everything but how he was going to take over his own life without regard to his father or anyone else.

CHAPTER 1

January 1816

The Duchess of Tunbridge had never been a jealous person. It wasn't in Bernadette's nature to covet what others had, nor guard her own possessions or relationships. Certainly, she'd never been one to turn ugly shades of green over the happiness of friends.

And yet she stood at the edge of a ballroom watching one of her dearest friends, Valaria, now the Duchess of Blackvale, dance at her wedding ball with her husband Callum, and Bernadette felt a stir of such an unpleasant emotion. She hated herself for it, because she knew what horrors Valaria had been through and how much she had earned her happy ending with her utterly devoted husband.

She turned away from them and her gaze caught her other best friend instead. Flora Desmond was not dancing with her husband, Roarke, but she, too, looked deliriously happy as they stood close together, their hands linked as they talked. Flora smiled, blushed a little when Roarke leaned in close to her ear.

Bernadette let out an unsteady sigh and moved away from the happy people celebrating and toward a long table where an alcoholic punch was being served. She took a glass, her third of the night, and swallowed a large mouthful before she got up the courage to turn her attention back to the room and all its happy couples. There was no escaping them, nor the way seeing them made her think and feel.

"That is a sour expression."

She jolted as she was joined in that vulnerable moment by yet another familiar face. Theodore Alexander Monroe Tinsley, the Duke of Lightmorrow, would likely call himself an old friend of hers. In fact, that was often how he introduced himself if they were together at some event. He wasn't incorrect. They had grown up on adjoining estates, after all. Their fathers had been friends and they had often seen each other over the years.

Her marriage to her late husband, the Duke of Tunbridge, had put distance between them. Theo's devotion to being an unattached rake had done the same. And yet they now often found each other thrown together thanks to the courtships and ultimately the marriages of their mutual friends.

"Good evening, Theo," she said, hoping she didn't sound as sour as he claimed she sounded.

"Etta," he drawled, and she stiffened as tingles moved up her spine both at the seductive tone to his voice and the fact that he used a shortened version of her name. He was the only person left on this earth who called her Etta.

She wasn't sure if she liked that or feared it and the reactions it caused in her.

"You aren't dancing," he said. "May I remedy that?"

She turned toward him to find his hand outstretched and anticipation on his expression. She felt a wild desire to refuse him, to run from the room and the feelings that touching him would inspire. This man made her weak and she knew it, even if she tried to ignore it.

But she couldn't do that, not without making a scene. She didn't need those ramifications. Certainly Callum and Valaria didn't either. So she swallowed down the rest of her punch, set her cup on a passing servant's tray and put her fingers against his palm. He was warm. She felt that through both their sets of thin gloves. He made no outward reaction to when she touched him, so she schooled her reaction in order to appear just as unmoved.

"Thank you, Your Grace," he said as he guided her to the floor and put his hand against her hip. They began to move together in a waltz and she cursed the universe that it would put her in this position where she had to look up into those dark brown eyes. Eyes that seemed to effortlessly see through everyone around him.

She cleared her throat. "Are you happy for Callum or lamenting his loss of freedom today?"

There was a moment when Bernadette thought she saw some version of regret cross Theo's face, but then it was gone and he smirked a little. God, but he was handsome. He was tall and broad shouldered, with smoldering dark brown eyes and thick brown hair. He was always perfectly groomed and dressed, and he always had the attention of every available woman in any room…and some portion of the attached ones, too. Even now ladies watched from every corner, glaring at her for having his interest, even briefly.

"A year or two ago, I admit I might have lamented about his being leg shackled, but I appear to be growing as a person."

She laughed at his playfully frustrated tone. As if growth were a bad thing. "God forbid," she teased. "So you would not say his marriage is a negative now?"

They pivoted, and Theo looked off to where Valaria and Callum now stood together. Callum's arm was around her waist, and while she spoke to someone, he was just…watching her, as if she were the most fascinating creature he'd ever encountered. And once again, Bernadette felt that pull of jealousy. What would it feel like to have someone look at her that way? To be so entirely focused on her and her happiness and her pleasure? She'd never experienced such a thing, certainly not with her own late husband.

Theo sighed. "He is besotted, and rightfully so. Valaria is not only beautiful, but she is a good match for him. No one could watch what they went through over the last year and not celebrate that they are finally free to be together." He winked at her and the seriousness of his tone melted away. "But if you tell anyone I said that, I will deny it."

"Of course, it will be our secret," she said, and forced a smile.

His brow wrinkled. "So we have established I am reluctantly happy for our friends," he said slowly. "Are you...are you not?" When she drew in a sharp breath, he hastened to add, "I have never seen you be anything but joyful for Valaria and Flora in their matches. But there is something about your expression. A little glumness at such a happy occasion that doesn't seem *you*."

Oh, how she hated how observant this man was. How much he could see through her without even trying, even though she meant nothing to him. He played at connection so easily that she couldn't trust it when she saw it shimmering there like a mirage.

"I'm...I'm not glum," she began, trying to meter her tone and knowing she failed when Theo's expression grew sharp.

Now all his focus was on her. "Etta?" he pressed, turning her gently in the crowd of dancers.

She stared up into those eyes and swallowed hard. The music was coming to an end and she needed to make her escape. She stepped from his arms as soon as she could and executed a curtsey. "Thank you for the dance, Theo," she said, and ducked away from him.

She heard him say her name as she left the dancefloor, but she kept going. She went straight through the crowd, as far from him as she could manage. Had it not been the dead of winter, she would have fled to the terrace, but all she could do now was hide as best she could.

Only he wouldn't let her. He pushed through the others toward her, his dark gaze locked on her. He paused only to grab two cups of punch from the table and then he came to her. He held out one to her as he arched a brow.

"You can't just run away in the middle of a conversation," he said. She shook her head. "If you were any kind of gentleman, you would have allowed my escape."

"A gentleman," he teased with a laugh. "Heaven forbid." His tone gentled. "What is it? What is troubling you?"

She sighed. He wouldn't let this go and as much as she knew she could keep it to herself, the words were right there on the tip of her tongue. Ready to wound if they were said to the wrong person. Perhaps it was better to say them to Theo and hope he would protect them.

"I'm happy for them," she whispered, and then drew in an unsteady breath. "But when I look at them it makes me...it makes me..."

"What?"

"Realize how alone I-I am," she stammered, each word heavy on her tongue.

"Ah," he said, and she couldn't help but notice how he angled himself away a fraction. The softness was gone. The connection loosened a little. It reminded her of another conversation they'd once shared, a lifetime ago. He'd turned away from her then, too. "Well, that is to be expected. You've been a widow for a while now, haven't you?"

"Five years," she said softly. "Almost twice as long as I was married in the first place."

"And you're young," he said carefully. "And attractive. Of course you would think about a marriage when all your friends were finding their match. It's natural you'd want that, Etta, and I'm...I'm sure you'll find someone."

She shook her head. He was saying the right things, she supposed. The same things Valaria and Flora would sometimes say, the same things her parents would say when she was forced to visit them once a month for icy, formal meetings. But when *Theo* said those words, it made her realize something and it bubbled from her lips before she could bid it back.

"It isn't a marriage that I desire," she whispered.

Now his eyes widened. "No?"

"I'm twenty-eight years old and you vastly overestimate my appeal to men looking for a match. Even if one wanted me like that, I don't need their money or their position. I have both of those things on my own. No, it's...it's the...the..." She shook her head again. "I suppose I wish that I could take a lover."

Theo had taken his own sip of punch, perhaps to look nonchalant as she stammered and struggled with the words to say something she should have kept to herself, but with that declaration he coughed and sent some portion of the drink bubbling from his lips.

He wiped the back of his hand across his mouth as he stared at her. "I beg your pardon?"

Oh, how she wished she could take that imprudent thought back now that she saw the horror on his face. He would see her differently after this. Their little friendship would change because he would know she was a wanton with lust on her mind.

"Never mind," she grunted, and pivoted to walk away again and find a quiet corner where she might be able to shrink into dust and blow apart on the wind.

He caught her elbow, tugging her back before him, and now he felt very close as he stared down at her, searching her face, his expression one of concern and...and something else. Something more heated. Something she had to be imagining when her veins were pumping with finally spoken desires and just enough punch to get her in trouble.

"You can't say something like that and just walk away, Etta," he said.

She flinched at his use, yet again, of the nickname. It made her feel special when he called her that and she knew she wasn't special. Not really. She pulled her arm away and folded them in an attempt to create a shield in front of herself.

"You needn't look so shocked," she choked out. "After all, I've heard the rumors about you. You don't ever lack a bed partner."

"It's…it's different," he murmured.

She lifted both brows. The alcohol in the punch was beginning to settle into her blood and it loosened her tongue more than she would have chosen to do. But here they were. "That's bollocks, Theo. Valaria and Flora prove that. Women have just as much passion and desire as men. So why wouldn't I want…want…a lover?"

He blinked at her. "I-I don't know what to say."

"You don't know what to say? *You* with all your vast experience and knowledge of pleasure? Surely you've bedded women like me."

He swallowed. "No, Etta, not like you."

Those words hit her like a slap and she physically turned her head at what felt like rejection. "Fine. So *you* would not want me. Well, I wasn't asking you to bed me by bringing this up. However…" She stared at him, thinking of all she'd ever heard about his wild behavior. "That doesn't mean you couldn't help."

"You want me to help you find a lover?" he gasped.

She flinched at the idea of this man she had fantasized about since she they were both young marching out and finding her a man to bed. A horrific idea. "I wouldn't ask that. But perhaps you would answer some questions that I have."

"Oh Christ," he muttered. "Bernadette."

She ignored his warning tone and the fact that he had reverted to calling her by her full name like she was a recalcitrant child. "For example, what do men want in a lover? How do you choose a lady to pursue for such things?"

With every question she asked, more popped into her head, and she found it impossible not to press him on them. After all, she'd already made a fool of herself, might as well get some vital information. Perhaps she would never pursue it, but now that the desire had been spoken, it was impossible to ignore.

"I can't—" he began.

She refused to allow him to continue. "Especially when you are taking on a relationship with someone of your own class?"

"Please—"

"How would someone like me protect their reputation? How do you ask for what you...what you want? Once you're to the bedding part, I mean? Do you just come out with it? Do you write a list of things you want to try or already know you don't like? Is it a negotiation?"

He stared at her, speechless, his mouth opening and closing like a fish. She might have crowed at her ability to stymie him, for she'd never known Theo not to have something to say. It was only humiliation that made it impossible to gloat. He almost looked...*horrified*...and that took the wind out of her slightly tipsy sails.

"There you are, Theo." Bernadette jumped at the sudden appearance of Callum at Theo's elbow. He gave a warm smile to Bernadette before he said, "May I steal him, Bernadette? We're doing a gentleman's toast in the billiard room."

"Of course," she breathed, and turned her face, as reality returned and sobered her. What had she been thinking? "Never mind what I was saying, Theo. Have a good night."

"I do want to talk to you about this," he said, but Callum was already dragging him away. Bernadette watched him go, watched him look back at her before he was taken from the room.

And she'd never felt quite so humiliated in her entire life.

Theo's ears were ringing as he stood in Callum's billiard room, surrounded by a handful of friends. He hadn't even heard the toast to his best friend's happiness, though he'd raised his glass in rote salute.

A life of excess meant he was not easily surprised, but his conversation with Etta had truly shocked him. He'd known her since they were both children and watched her in the years since.

He'd always seen her as sweet and soft, kind and comforting. Those qualities had drawn him to her, for they were so opposite to how he saw himself.

But now she had looked him in the eye and asked...asked for something he'd never allowed himself to believe she would desire.

"You looked shocked," Roarke Desmond said as he approached with Callum at his side.

Roarke was a new addition to their small circle of friends, but Theo liked him. He was intelligent and shared a similar sense of humor to Theo and Callum, who had been friends since they were in school what felt like a lifetime ago.

Callum chuckled. "He does," he said. "Is the happiness of your friends so terrifying?"

Theo knew they were teasing and normally he would have played along, but right now his head was spinning so his answer was a bit sharper than he would have normally made it. "No."

Callum's forehead wrinkled but he didn't back off. Of course he didn't. "Ah, then perhaps you are ready to follow us into wedded bliss."

Theo continued to try to catch his breath and Roarke laughed. "He has no words. Good show, Blackvale!"

Theo shook his head to try to clear it. Right now he was a jumble of thoughts and he didn't want to share any of them with his friends. What had happened with Etta was between them, no one else needed to know about it. Especially since she would certainly have different thoughts once she wasn't in high emotion, once she wasn't a little tipsy from punch.

"It isn't you, you two idiots," he said with a forced laugh. "Come, I haven't toasted the groom yet." He lifted a glass and smiled at the room. "Let me tell you all about the *real* Blackvale."

The other gentleman around them made raucous *ohhs* and Theo launched into a few amusing stories of their misspent youth, but all the while he kept thinking about Etta. He was going to have to address what had happened between them, he would have to figure out how later.

If he could.

CHAPTER 2

Bernadette's head hurt as she sat having tea with Valaria and Flora the next day. She wanted to say it was all because of too much punch, and a great deal of it was. But partly it was because she hadn't been able to sleep the night before. All she could think of was Theo's reaction when she'd declared her desire to take a lover.

He'd walked away and hadn't returned to her, despite his claim that he wished to speak further on the subject. She'd hardly even seen him afterward at the party, almost as if he were avoiding her. And she hated that she'd created a situation when she could have just kept her thoughts to herself.

"Would you like more tea, Valaria?" Flora asked.

Valaria was staring at her plate, a little smile on her face, and she jolted at her name. "What?"

Flora giggled and nudged Bernadette from her own thoughts. "Look at her. She's so bleary-eyed and with a dreamy expression. It seems as though your wedding night went well."

Bernadette smiled and it wasn't forced. Valaria and Callum had rushed to their marriage the moment it was socially acceptable to do so, which meant their wedding tour was slightly delayed. They would go in just a handful of days for what sounded like a wonderful time alone together.

"It isn't as if Valaria and Callum haven't been having wedding nights for months before," Bernadette said, "But oh my, you do look like you enjoyed yourself, my dear."

Valaria blushed now, all the way down to below the neckline of her gown. "Stop, you two!" she said with a joyful laugh.

"We shall not," Flora declared. "Tell us, was it different as his wife than it has been as his secret lover?"

Valaria let out a long sigh and clutched her hands at her breast. "It was wonderful. It's always wonderful, he makes everything wonderful the moment he touches me. But last night I was his wife at last and he claimed me like I was."

"Oh, I felt the same way with Roarke after we went to Gretna Green last year," Flora said with a dreamy sigh. "I know some women complain about their husbands as lovers, but it only gets better and better."

Bernadette blushed at those words. Her friends were discussing the very passion she was trying to address with Theo the night before. The passion she had never experienced and now was drawn to so powerfully.

Valaria nodded. "Sometimes I think of how hard I fought to keep him away and shudder to think what I would have lost."

"I'm so happy for you both," Bernadette said, and the words drew their attention to her. They both faced her and she shifted beneath their regard. She could feel the edges of their pity and she feared it. It was part of the reason she hadn't addressed her desire to take a lover with them.

"How long until your place here on Kent's Row is empty?" she asked Valaria as a way to avoid any questions she didn't want to answer.

Now Valaria's expression grew sad and she and Flora exchanged a glance once more. Flora had been gone for months from her place on the Row where the women had all been neighbors. Bernadette had other friends on the street, of course, which was populated with widows, mostly. But they were older ladies, not interested in some of the lively things she and these two discussed.

"Only a few days more," Valaria said in answer to the question. Tears flooded her eyes. "It was a refuge for me when I came here. You two were and are a refuge. And as happy as I am to finally be able to live under the same roof as my love, I will miss our times together here."

Bernadette caught her hand and squeezed gently. "And will you sell it, as Flora did with her place?"

"Yes," Valaria said slowly.

Bernadette got up and crossed to the sideboard, where she poured herself more tea without looking at them. "Well, it all makes sense, of course," she choked out. She felt them move toward her even before both of them wrapped their arms around her from behind.

"We hate leaving you!" Flora sobbed.

Bernadette turned into her friends, and for a moment they were a blubbering mess together. But at last she wiped at her tears and tried to put on a good face. "You aren't leaving me, of course. We'll see each other often. I am capable of going across Town to your neighborhoods and you will come here." She smoothed her skirt. "And new ladies will come to the Row. Though I do have to say that the dowager who took Flora's old place moved in last week, and I swear all she wanted to talk about when we met was fox hunting. More specifically, fox hunts she went on twenty-five years ago." She pulled a face and Flora and Valaria smiled.

"You know," Valaria said as she motioned them all back to the sitting area in the middle of Bernadette's parlor. "You could let a place farther into Town. Nearer to both of us."

Bernadette bent her head. "No, I've settled here. The idea of moving all over again seems…" She trailed off. She didn't want to say *pathetic* for fear it would rouse a whole conversation she wasn't prepared to have. Instead she lifted her chin and smiled. "But

Valaria, have you managed to wheedle out of Callum where he intends to take you for your honeymoon in a few days?"

"Yes," Flora encouraged. "I wondered that too. The weather looks to cooperate despite the season."

They began to talk about that, with Valaria giving her guesses. Despite her own maudlin thoughts, Bernadette lost herself in their laughter and joy. She didn't begrudge them their happiness. In fact, she welcomed it. But she still couldn't help but feel like they were two wives...and she was the one left behind. The unwanted one.

She thought again of Theo's expression of horror when she'd said she wanted a lover and blushed despite her attempts not to react.

"Are you *certain* you're well?" Valaria asked, covering her hand.

"I'm fine," she lied, and hoped that would make it true.

Flora didn't look convinced, but she sipped her tea. "Are you still going through those boxes in the attic?"

"Yes," Bernadette said, relieved to discuss something that didn't feel laced with emotion. "I realized that some of Tunbridge's things were packed along with mine. Letters, it seems, so I'll need to go through them and see what can be destroyed and if anything needs to be returned for the family."

Flora flinched. "Oh, I'm sorry. That must be a difficult task."

Now it was Bernadette who exchanged a look with Valaria. Flora's first marriage had been a happy one, so she sometimes didn't understand the indifference one could feel toward a late spouse. She shrugged. "I don't think it will be. He wasn't a particularly interesting man. I'm certain it's all entirely boring."

Like her life, actually. And she hated that it was so true. That it might always be true.

~

Theo paced his study, wishing he could pretend away the subject that troubled his mind. Only he couldn't. He hadn't for nearly twenty-four hours.

Etta. He could only think of Etta and her shocking statement that she wished to take a lover. He'd thought about it the entire remainder of the ball last night, watching her even as he avoided her so he could *think*.

Then his betrayer of a mind had conjured dreams of her, head thrown back, dark hair down around her shoulders, face contorted in pleasure as she rode...a lover. Him. Rode him. And he'd woken up hard as steel and aching for her.

He'd tried to push the thoughts aside the rest of the day, but they would not go. She haunted every corner of his existence now, her words echoing in his mind. Her expression rising up before him when he was trying to do literally anything else but ponder her and her desires.

"Shit," he grunted as he pivoted to pace once more. He stared at his door as he came to a stop. Perhaps the best thing he could do now was actually talk to her. Unlike last night, she would be fully sober now, certainly she would tell him what she'd said was a mistake. He would reassure her, they would go back to the friendship they had rekindled when Valaria and Callum's affair and subsequent marriage had thrown them back together after years apart.

Everything could go back to normal. He knew it was true.

He exited the room and called out to his butler that he would not be home for supper. Kimball didn't seem surprised—after all, Theo often didn't remain home for meals. He went out into the world. Sought pleasure.

Not tonight, of course. He wasn't going to seek pleasure with Etta.

"Shit," he repeated as he strode down to the stable and waited for his horse to be prepared.

The ride to Kent's Row was a quarter of an hour and he tried to quiet his mind as he took it. Tried to make himself look unaffected as he turned into her drive and stared up at her home. He could see her through the window in her parlor that looked out over the street. She was standing by the fire, reading a letter. His heart beat a little faster.

"Shit," he said again, and thought, briefly, about simply riding away and never returning ever again. Only her servants had begun to swarm and he couldn't do so. So instead he swung down from his mount and made his way up the stairs to where her butler awaited him.

"Your Grace," he intoned.

"I realize I am not expected," Theo said. "But will you see if the duchess will see me?"

There was a brief change to the man's expression that Theo didn't entirely understand, but then he inclined his head. "A moment, Your Grace."

He disappeared and Theo hated that his heart throbbed faster as he waited. Would she see him? Or was she so embarrassed by what had happened between them the night before that she would pretend she wasn't available? And then what would he do? Stride down the hall and press his suit? Or break away from her and never see her again? Make things awkward for their friends? For her? For himself?

Luckily he didn't have to come up with those answers, for the butler returned and motioned him toward the parlor where he'd seen Etta earlier. "Her Grace will see you."

The relief Theo felt was too powerful and he entered the room entirely out of sorts. A feeling that didn't ease when she turned from the fire and he caught his breath. She was no longer holding the letter she'd been reading when he arrived and she smoothed her skirt gently. God, but she was pretty. So bloody pretty that he wanted to hold this image of her forever in his mind. Conjure it when he needed a little light in his life.

"Theo," she said, stepping toward him hesitantly. She gripped her hands in and out of fists at her sides. "I...I didn't expect you."

He somehow found breath enough to speak. "My apologies. I should have sent word ahead, but my decision to come here was rather sudden." He moved closer and watched her pupils dilate, her hands shake a little before she gripped them again. "I can't stop thinking about what you said to me last night."

Her eyes went wide and a dark flush entered her cheeks and spread down the exposed flesh of her throat into the sloped neckline of her pretty blue dress. "Oh?"

"Did you mean what you said to me?" he asked. She hesitated again and her gaze left his. He pursed his lips. "Etta."

"I suppose my humiliation must be complete," she murmured, he thought more to herself than to him. She lifted her eyes and held his gaze evenly. "If you were any other person in the world, I could play this off. I could pretend I didn't recall what I said. I could say I meant something else. I could lie. But not with you."

"Not with me?" he repeated. "Why?"

"Because you see through me," she said, her tone suddenly faraway. "I feel you always have."

He opened and shut his mouth at that statement. It was odd, because he'd always felt that way about her. Even as a girl, she had pulled things from him that he wouldn't have shared, never had shared, with anyone else. When they'd been reunited with Callum and Valaria's union, he'd hoped Etta wouldn't have that power anymore.

But she did. Still. Always. He should have run from it, but he hadn't.

"So you *do* want to take a lover," he pressed, and heard how rough his voice had become. She nodded silently and just like the night before, her response seemed to weave its way into his flesh, his bone, his blood. It conjured images so inappropriate that he had to turn away from her so they wouldn't be so clear.

JESS MICHAELS

"I do worry about your safety," he mused as he stared out the window.

"Oh," she said from behind him. He heard disappointment in that tiny word. "Of course that would be your concern. It's very kind of you, Theo, but it's not your responsibility. You can disabuse yourself of that notion."

He faced her again just in time to see her moving toward the door. Perhaps she intended to ring for tea, perhaps she meant to excuse him from her presence. Either way, he recognized she wanted to create a distraction so this conversation could be over and he couldn't allow that.

He moved to her in a few long steps and caught her arm. She staggered back against his chest and looked up at him with a gasp. Oh, that gasp. He so very much wanted to make her make that sound for far more pleasurable purposes.

She blinked. "Th-Theo, I'm not asking you to want me. I know you don't, I would never burden you that way. Honestly I'm not even sure I could find *anyone* to want me, so there may be no point to this entire exercise."

He stared at her now, bewildered for a new reason. "You cannot be serious."

She tugged her arm away and stepped back, smoothing her skirt over and over. "It's a serious subject—of course I'm being serious. I know what I am and what I'm not. And I realize I'm being an utter fool, perhaps."

"You think no one would want you?" he repeated.

She lifted her chin. "No one ever has."

"Your husband," he retorted, folding his arms.

She mirrored the action, clearly intending to use her arms as a shield. Something to hide from him behind. But he saw the pain flash across her face, she wasn't a practiced enough liar to hide it.

Not like him.

"No," she admitted. "He didn't want me."

The shield she had wished to crate slipped further, because in

24

that moment Theo saw everything. Her marriage had been arranged. It was a topic they had discussed years ago, in a few stolen moments on the worst birthday of his life. But when her engagement had been announced, Theo had been certain that Tunbridge would come to care for her. Certainly the duke would want her. Theo hadn't wasted a lot of time picturing their marriage, but he'd had a fleeting moment where he considered the other man lucky to have Etta.

And now he could see that hadn't been true. He did see through her, as she claimed he could, and what he saw was loneliness, sorrow, loss. It called to his own and he let out a shuddering breath. It called to his guilt in the circumstances she'd found herself in all those years and he almost couldn't take another.

"Oh," he whispered, and ran a hand through his hair. She turned away as he did, her shoulders rolled forward, her breath a little shallow. He couldn't leave her like this, imprudent as what he was going to say next was. "Please look at me."

"Why?" she asked, and her tone was a touch forlorn.

"Because I want you to know I mean what I'm about to say," he said.

She turned slowly and looked up at him. "Go ahead."

"It isn't about not wanting you, Etta. Not for me and not for anyone else." Her gaze fluttered over him and he forced himself to continue. "I've seen men watch you many times. I-I've watched you. You *are* wanted. But the greater question is, what do *you* want?"

She was trembling now, those dark eyes so wide that they were all he could see. "I-I—" she struggled.

He moved closer once more. Now he was almost touching her again. God, how he wanted to touch her. "If you can't even say what you want—" he began.

She pushed her shoulders back. "I want to feel desired, Theo. I want to feel alive."

His breath caught. Oh, how he knew that feeling. And he knew that chasing pleasure wouldn't quite get one there, no matter how hard one tried. At least not permanently. But then again, she wasn't talking about permanently. And he could no longer resist her temptation.

He reached out and drew her fingertips along her jawline. He had touched her before, but never like this.

"Theo," she whispered, almost imperceptibly despite the fact they were practically in each other's arms.

He tilted her chin up, watched her lips part on a shaky sigh. And then he did he thing he realized he'd been waiting a lifetime to do: he kissed her.

B ernadette had pictured kissing Theo before. She'd done so as a lonely young woman who couldn't stop looking at him whenever she was near. She'd even done so as a married lady, when she watched him dance by with someone else in his arms. She'd pictured it all.

And it was nothing compared to the reality when his lips met hers, soft at first, just a featherlight touch, and then with more firmness. His tongue darted out, traced the crease of her lips, and she opened to him on a sigh she couldn't control. He took then, delving deep as his arms came around her waist and he drew her against him. She lifted against his chest, feeling the warmth of him, reveling in the taste of him, sinking into the sensation of their tongues and breath mingling.

Everything Flora and Valaria giggled about together, everything in naughty books, *everything* made sense now as she wrapped her arms around his neck and whimpered at the pleasure of this touch. It woke such a longing in her, a desire that made what she'd felt before seem like nothing more than a trickle. This was a waterfall. An ocean. She wanted to drown in it.

He angled his head, pressing the fingers of one hand up into her hair to hold her steady as he kissed her even more deeply. It was as if he claimed her with this seemingly simple act. As if he marked her in some way she wouldn't forget, even if no one else saw it. She would know a part of her was his and would be his forever.

But as quickly as it had begun, as surely as he had swept her away, he broke from her. He stepped back as he released her, holding up his hands as if to show her he wasn't touching her anymore. His expression was wild and untethered, uncertain and possessive all at once.

"Forgive me," he ground out, his voice raw and rough as he pivoted on his heel and staggered from the room.

She heard him leave, heard the door slam behind him, and she sank into the closest chair, her hands shaking, her heart throbbing and her entire being bombarded by feelings and sensations.

The greatest of which was giddy excitement. This was what she'd wanted, what she'd dreamed of having when she thought of taking a lover. And until that moment, she hadn't been certain she would like it so much. But she had. And she wanted more. She wanted all of it.

She wanted it with Theo, if she was honest with herself. But the fact that he had run from her didn't bode well. After all, he could have any woman in the world, whatever he said about watching her or wanting her, there were far greater options for him.

But that didn't mean she had no options, herself.

She opened a small drawer on the side table next to the settee and drew out the letter she had been reading when her butler, Waterstone, had announced Theo. It was one of the things she'd found in her late husband's things as she cleaned out her attic. She'd expected messages from friends and business associates, and had intended to return the messages to those they had come from or hand over anything that could have meaning to Tunbridge's remaining family.

But this letter…it had drawn her up short. It was from a man named Paul Abbot, who seemed to manage an underground club called the Donville Masquerade. The message, dated just a few weeks before Tunbridge's death, was a reprimand to her husband, who had apparently broken a rule of the club.

As you well know, the Donville Masquerade highly encourages open displays of passion. Its members may play together privately or in public in any way that brings pleasure. However, Your Grace, the forcefulness in which you approached your partner last week was not welcome. And though you did eventually acquiesce when she said no, the matter must be resolved with a ban of one year from the establishment without refund of your membership dues. You may reapply once your ban has ended, though your acceptance is not guaranteed.

She shifted. She might not have as much experience as Theo did or apparently as her husband did…she understood this letter wasn't referring to a usual club. The use of *passion* and *pleasure* in the note made her think it was something more. A place where members could *play*, which she believed from context must have to do with sin.

She shivered at the idea.

And also felt sick that her husband had maintained such a presence there. Not only could he have slaked needs there that he refused to bring to her, but it sounded like he hadn't always pursued partners who were willing. She was spinning from that knowledge. Perhaps that was part of why she'd been so open with Theo. She needed whatever steadiness he could provide.

And she also needed to understand the past. If she went to this place, perhaps she could understand more about what her late husband had been doing, as well as determine what the club was at all and if she might, herself, have a place there. Because if Theo didn't want to be the one to provide escape, pleasure…well, then wouldn't a place like this Donville Masquerade be as good a place as any to try to find a partner who would?

Perhaps if that were true, it would be an even better outlet for her desires. Because a willing stranger wouldn't make her *feel* so much as Theo did. In the end, it might be much less dangerous. If only she could will herself to do it.

CHAPTER 3

The building Bernadette had convinced her driver to take her to at three the next afternoon was not what she expected. It was rather plain, something one could easily drive right past without ever noticing it. And yet when her footman opened the door for her, he appeared worried.

"Your Grace," he said. "Are you certain—"

"Yes," she said, a bit sharper than she intended. "I have questions for the proprietor of this establishment and I intend to get answers. I appreciate your concern, but it's not warranted."

The servant didn't look convinced, but he inclined his head regardless and helped her down. As she moved forward, the door opened and a tall, large man stood there. "The club isn't open until nine," he said, firmly but not unkindly.

She shifted. Every fiber of her being urged her to turn heel and go home, but wasn't that what she'd been doing all her life? If she wanted something more for her future, if she wanted a chance for more of what she'd felt with Theo when he'd kissed her, she had no choice but to be brave.

"Ah, I see," she said. "But...But I am not here to attend the club. I have business with the owner."

"Mr. Rivers is...indisposed," the man grunted.

She folded her arms. "Is there no manager? No one a lady could speak to on behalf of a late patron?"

The man's gaze moved down her body in an appraising manner, though not in a way that made her uncomfortable. Then he let out a long sigh. "Very well. Follow me."

She could have crowed she was so pleased with herself for not backing down as she usually did. Somehow she merely followed the man inside instead. There was a vestibule just inside the door and beyond it an intricately carved door. The man motioned for her to take a seat just next to where she'd entered.

"I'll see if Mr. Abbot will take a moment for you. What is your name?"

A cold shiver worked through her. Once she gave her name, there was no going back. "The Duchess of Tunbridge," she said softly.

His eyebrows lifted. "I see. Please wait."

He went through the carved door and she pushed to her feet almost immediately. There was a high table near the second entrance with an unlit lamp, a quill pen and closed ink bottle. There was space there for a book or papers, she assumed to check memberships, but there was nothing there to snoop in, much to her chagrin. She had to wonder what kind of people had memberships to this place, if its activities were what she believed they might be. What kind of person did it make *her* that she was so titillated by the idea?

She turned toward the inner door and leaned closer to look at the carvings. When she did, she gasped. They were wooden images, in great detail, of demons and angels in the midst of very erotic behaviors. Two by two, three together, even a pile of bodies, writhing in pleasure.

When the door opened, she yelped and staggered back. She was greeted by a tall, wiry man. He was handsome but had an unreadable expression as he looked at her. "Your Grace?" he queried.

She nodded. "Y-yes. Are you Mr. Abbot?"

"I am. Habor says you came inquiring after your late husband."

She blinked. "I…how did you know he was dead?"

"He was a public figure, Your Grace." He smiled slightly. "And my job here is to know everything."

"Good." She drew in an unsteady breath. "Then you could perhaps tell me more about his time at this establishment."

There was a flutter of pity that crossed Mr. Abbot's face. "I apologize, Your Grace, but I cannot give you any information."

"You don't know it or you won't share it?" she asked.

"The second," Abbot said without hesitation. "You see, a club such as this one can only survive with the greatest of discretion. I can't share any details about anyone who comes here, no matter what their relationship is or *was* to the questioner."

Her lips parted. "I see."

"I apologize that you came all the way here. I wish you had written," Abbot said. "I would not have had you waste your time." He motioned toward the door and Bernadette's heart began to pound.

"Do you offer memberships to women?" The words fell from her lips in an almost jumbled way.

Mr. Abbott seemed to understand them regardless, for he lowered his hand. "Yes."

"W-women like…like m-me?" she pressed.

He smiled slightly. "There are women of title who hold membership here, yes, Your Grace. Is that what you meant?"

She was still trying to digest that fact and she blinked at him. "Y-Yes. And what would it take for *me* to join?"

He had the same uncertain expression her footman and her driver had each had when she mentioned the name of this place. Her heart sank. He didn't think her the right material.

"I can be discreet," she burst out. "And I won't bother anyone. I'm a member of several charitable societies if you require references and—"

"Paul."

JESS MICHAELS

Bernadette jerked her gaze over toward the female voice that had spoken from the main entrance to the club. A pretty, petite woman with chestnut-brown hair piled artfully atop the crown of her head was standing at the now-open door, hands clasped before her.

"Yes, Mrs. Rivers," Abbot said with a slight incline of his head.

"Marcus was looking for you," Mrs. Rivers said softly. "Why don't you let me handle the duchess?"

Mr. Abbot nodded. "Of course." He smiled at Bernadette kindly. "Good day, Your Grace."

He slipped past the pretty woman into the club. Once they were alone, Mrs. Rivers stepped forward. "Do you know who I am?"

Bernadette examined her more closely and then took in a quick breath. "I-I do. You're Lady Annabelle. You're the sister of the Duke of Hartholm."

"I am Annabelle Rivers," the other woman said gently. "My brother *is* the Duke of Hartholm, but no one calls me Lady Annabelle anymore, unless it is my husband choosing to tease me mercilessly."

There was a tone in which she said that which made Bernadette think the lady didn't mind such teasing much. "We weren't out at the same time," Bernadette said. "I was married the year you made your debut."

"But I'm sure you heard the whispers when *I* married Marcus two years ago," Mrs. Rivers said. "How I married a scoundrel." Bernadette shifted under the truth of that statement and Mrs. Rivers grinned. "It's quite all right, Your Grace. I know *they* talk. My husband owns this establishment. Won't you come in and we can talk more comfortably than in this drafty entryway?"

Bernadette nodded, shocked that she would be so easily allowed access to this mysterious place when a few moments before she was almost begging for it. She followed Mrs. Rivers through the scandalously carved door and into a huge room filled with tables, chairs and various settees and other couches. There was a large bar in the back, but it was far finer and brighter than any pub bar she'd seen during travel on the roads.

"Oh, it's beautiful, Mrs. Rivers," she breathed.

"Thank you, but you must call me Annabelle."

Bernadette looked at the young woman again. She had a kind face and didn't seem to be preparing to do anything nefarious or cruel. "Bernadette," she said softly.

"Bernadette," Annabelle replied. "Come, Marcus and Paul are working on something in one of our back rooms, so our office is available."

She led Bernadette up a back stair and into a big room with a huge swath of windows that overlooked the club below. "Oh!" Bernadette gasped as she took in the vast, bird's eye view of every corner of the room.

"Marcus takes a hands-on involvement. Will you have something to drink? I have tea and something stronger."

"No," Bernadette said as she settled into a comfortable leather seat across from the desk where Annabelle settled herself. She cleared her throat. "I suppose you did not come here back when my husband did. But perhaps *you* know about him and his activities here?"

Annabelle pursed her lips. "Paul was correct when he told you that discretion does not allow such discussion. I'm sorry if that hurts you, but the truth might hurt even more."

"I see," Bernadette sighed. Of course, as much as her curiosity was unsatisfied, she knew in her heart that asking about Tunbridge's behavior hadn't really been why she came here. It was just an excuse to get her into the carriage.

"I brought you here because I heard you ask Paul if you might take a membership and I thought that it might be better to discuss such a thing woman to woman."

Bernadette nodded slowly. "Very well."

Annabelle leaned back in the chair and steepled her fingers. "Are you fully aware of what kind of club this is?"

"From the letter I found regarding my husband, I gleaned that it is some kind of place of pleasure. A bawdy house, perhaps? Or something like it?"

"Not exactly," Annabelle said. "Our Society is so restricted. We are forced to conform to so many rules of behavior and desire that people need a place with more freedom. The Donville Masquerade provides that. People come here, my dear, for sex. They game like at other hells, and some of our entertainments are slightly more... wholesome. But the reason people pay for membership and come here rather than anywhere else is because they like to play. Do you understand what that means?"

"That term was in the letter I found," Bernadette whispered. "I don't know."

Annabelle leaned forward. "In a few hours the club will open. And that big room we came through will fill up with men and women. And they will touch each other. Kiss and rub and sometimes—oh, I hate to use this word since you are a lady, but I want you to understand—fuck. They'll do it in public, they'll do it in the rooms in the back, they'll watch others do it to become excited."

Bernadette stared at her, slack jawed as those words sank in. "Oh," she squeaked.

"We *do* offer membership to anyone who agrees to follow the rules and can pay the fee. However, I wouldn't want you to waste your money if you thought this was just some regular gaming facility or a stuffy club like you'd find in other parts of London."

And there it was. Like a fork in the road, Bernadette saw the path of her life diverge into two places. One went back to those stuffy clubs and charitable societies and empty halls of her empty house.

And the other went to a place where Annabelle had described remarkable, erotic, terrifying things. Things Bernadette hadn't even begun to fully imagine when she declared she wanted a lover.

But if there were anyplace to find one...wouldn't a place like this be it? She wouldn't have to ask for Theo's help anymore or face his rejection. She wouldn't risk emotion with his kiss if he chose to ever bestow it again. She could find a lover, get the deed done, and know what it was like to be desired.

"I want a membership," she whispered, her voice breaking.

Annabelle's eyebrows lifted as if she were surprised, but then she smiled. "As you wish."

She opened a drawer in front of her and pulled out a ledger. Slowly, she thumbed through it, skimming names and notes scribbled in the margins in a tight, disciplined hand. Eventually she looked up at Bernadette.

"I've found your late husband's membership information," she said.

Bernadette blinked. "You intend to tell me something about him now?"

"No, I wanted to see how much he'd had left on his membership when he was...er..."

"Banned," Bernadette said. "I know he was banned for a year for some incident."

"Yes. Well, he had just paid for a five-year membership at the time of his removal," Annabelle said. "When fees like that are forfeited, they go into a fund to support members in good standing who might need a little help, or for courtesans and lightskirts who come here looking for safety in performing their arts."

Bernadette drew back. "I see."

"However, I see no problem in allowing some of that fund to pass to you for a shorter membership to see if you'd like to continue."

Bernadette blinked at that unexpected kindness. "Why would you do that?"

Annabelle's mouth pinched a little. "I assume this man was as unkind to you as he might have been within these walls. Only you didn't have the power to ban him as we did."

Bernadette bent her head and pushed away thoughts of how needlessly and casually cruel her late husband could be. Just for fun.

He'd never been physical, but he'd always made sure she knew how utterly unwanted she was.

"He would hate that I was here," she said softly.

"Then all the more reason to do it." Annabelle turned the ledger several pages and began to write. "This ledger is private—only Marcus and I, and Mr. Abbot, have access to it, so you will have no fear that you'd be exposed for membership by us."

"Then how will anyone know I have a membership when I come to the door?" Bernadette asked.

"You will have a name you give at the door that will be on the list," Annabelle explained. "Something you can remember and will answer to, but won't be something most people know you by. Do you have an idea of what to call yourself?"

She cleared her throat. Only one name came to mind, and damn it all, but it made her think of the very man she was trying to forget as part of this. "Etta," she whispered.

"Etta," Annabelle repeated.

It seemed almost wrong to hear someone other than Theo call her that name. No one else had for so long that it rang in her ears. She nodded nonetheless. "Yes."

"Very good." Annabelle scribbled a few things in the entry for her membership and then closed the ledger. She came around the desk and leaned on the corner. In the breath before she spoke again, Bernadette took her in. There was something so certain about this woman. So sure in herself and her role. Bernadette wished she could be so strong.

"A few rules to review before we are finished," Annabelle said. "Firstly, this club is meant for sexual pleasure and anything goes... but only between consenting partners. You are allowed to say no to anything at any time. You are not allowed to pursue if the other partner says no."

Bernadette thought of the letter to Tunbridge and blushed. "I understand."

"You may not ever speak about what you see here to anyone

outside of these walls. People come here for privacy, so even if you identify someone you know, this must never be spoken of."

"I would not want someone to talk about my being here, so I wouldn't do the same to anyone else."

Annabelle nodded. "Very good. Now, to protect your own identity, we recommend wearing a mask. It isn't required and you may see some without one, but it's the best way to remain anonymous in any…encounter."

"Oh, that's why you call it the Donville Masquerade!" Bernadette said with a laugh, though her stomach fluttered at the idea of an anonymous encounter. It was so wicked.

And it would also solve the problem of being unwanted. No one would know it was her. So she could be anyone she desired to be. It would be safe. Or as safe as one could expect.

Annabelle pushed off from the edge of the desk with a smile. "You'll be reminded of these things when you arrive. The club opens at nine, but I'd recommend coming after ten so that you get the full experience. And I do not wear a mask while I circulate, so if you ever need anything, please find me or ask for me."

"I will," Bernadette said, practically bouncing as she was led down the stairs and back out into the main hell. There, Annabelle extended a hand.

"Habor will call for your carriage if it's not outside the door," she explained. "I hope to see you soon."

"Thank you," Bernadette said as the two women shook hands. "For your help and your kindness."

"Of course."

Annabelle smiled at her once more, and then the two women turned from each other and went their separate ways. But at the exit into the vestibule, she turned back and saw Annabelle walk up to a very tall, broadly built man. He caught her hand and drew her up short and hard against his chest. Annabelle laughed and then lifted up on her tiptoes so the two could kiss passionately before the club door closed and she could no longer see them.

Bernadette felt the heat in her cheeks as she turned away and hustled forward to wait for her carriage. The kiss reminded her too much of Theo, but he had left. He had apologized for kissing her. So she had to focus on the future, not the past.

And her future, at present, was a return to this place later that night.

CHAPTER 4

Theo couldn't have named exactly how many times he'd thought about getting on his horse and riding back to Bernadette's in the time since he'd left her. But it was more than ten. He kept trying to convince himself he would just talk to her about the kiss that never should have happened. That he would just settle the situation between them and help them return to friends.

But he never went, and it was because he knew what would actually happen was that he would kiss her all over again and this time he wouldn't be able to stop himself. He would ruin everything and eventually she would despise him for it.

"Mr. Desmond, Your Grace," Kimball said from his study door, and Theo turned from the window where he had been doing his brooding and forced a welcoming smile as his friend entered the room.

He'd known Roarke since their time at Eton, and then the acquaintance had been renewed a few months before. Theo liked the man, and he respected him. Roarke had been taken under the wing of noted industrialist Grayson Danford and had been doing very well for himself in the months since.

"And there you are. I hope you're here to tell me that my investment in all this steam nonsense is already paying off," Theo said as he crossed the room, hand outstretched.

"It is, indeed," Roarke said. He accepted the whisky that Theo poured him before the two of them sat down and had a good conversation about the innovations that might one day make steam engines the norm. Half of the science Theo didn't understand, but one couldn't help but be swept up in Roarke's enthusiasm.

At last he settled back in his chair and looked Theo up and down. "Anything I can do to help?" he asked.

Theo blinked. One of the things he liked most about this man was that he couldn't yet see through him like Callum could. And somehow here he was, doing just that.

"Help?" he repeated with a humorless laugh. "What would I need help with?"

"I don't know," Roarke admitted. "There's just something about your expression."

"Ah yes," Theo said, keeping his tone light. "What you are seeing is the peaceful countenance of a man who is not leg shackled. You may not recognize it since you and Callum have both succumbed to societal expectation."

Roarke laughed, which was the purpose of the joke, but he said, "You know, you might not hate it as much as you think. I believe the duke and I are very *happily* leg shackled."

Theo thought of Etta's mouth beneath his own. The little sound she'd made when his tongue touched hers. He pushed those images away along with images of her looking up at him all those years ago, making him wish for...

"I suppose we'll never know," he said, staring into his drink. "I don't intend to marry until I'm eighty-two and then only to produce an heir."

"At eighty-two," Roarke said with a shake of his head. "What a feat." They were both quiet a moment and then he said, "Are you certain you have nothing you need to discuss?"

"Nothing at all." Theo got up and moved back to the window he had abandoned. "If I seem maudlin to you, I suppose I'm just being…being foolish. What I need to do is clear my head. Go out and have a bit of fun. Usually I'd drag Callum along for such adventures, but he's busy at the moment. Would you like to join me?"

Roarke got up and set his empty glass aside. "It's a kind offer, but I also have plans with my wife."

Theo's brow wrinkled. In a flash of a moment he realized that now that his friends were both married and unfashionably in love with their wives…he was left out. No longer part of the center of the inner circle. And so was Bernadette. Perhaps that was why they were suddenly drawn to each other.

Once again, he shook those thoughts away. "Well, you enjoy that. Perhaps I'll go to the Donville Masquerade. It's been a while and it's always a fine distraction."

Roarke held his gaze a moment too long and then shrugged. "You have a good time."

Theo saw him out, but as he watched his friend ride down the drive, the idea of the Donville Masquerade didn't feel very good. It felt like he was living a lie. And betraying a woman he had already refused.

If Annabelle had tried to prepare her with harsh language, Bernadette still hadn't fully understood what she was in for. But now she stood in the middle of the Donville Masquerade, wearing a blue satin mask she had hastily stitched with paste pearls earlier in the day, watching everything around her in overwhelmed awe.

All around her was noise and color and sin. She'd been at the masquerade for all of twenty minutes and she'd already seen so many people doing so many sensual things with and to each other. Kissing in ways that would cause a scandal in a proper house, dancing with not an inch between them as hands roved freely, and more. Things her husband had certainly never done to her.

She lifted a hand to touch her mask, to ensure her face was still covered. Although Annabelle had promised her that this was a safe space, she wasn't fully certain of it yet. And if the wrong person discovered she was here and *wasn't* discreet, it could be disastrous for her reputation. At any rate, she didn't feel entirely protected by a thin layer of satin and frivolity.

"You look nervous, Miss Etta."

Bernadette pivoted and found Annabelle Rivers standing at her side. "Oh, Annabelle, you scared me."

"Yes, you looked a little lost and I thought I'd come say good evening." Together they looked out over the hall at all the debauchery. "May I ask you a question that I didn't want to pry about earlier in the day?"

The way that statement was couched made Bernadette nervous, but how could she refuse to answer the woman who had granted her entry? "Certainly."

"Why did you want to come here?" Annabelle asked gently. "Was it only to find out about what your husband did or didn't do all those years ago?"

Bernadette shifted. "No," she finally admitted slowly. "Honestly, when it comes to his betrayals of me, I wasn't surprised. His disregard was no mystery, even before I knew he took his appetites elsewhere. And he's been dead long enough that sometimes I don't even recall his face."

"So you did truly come for yourself." Annabelle reached out and squeezed her hand when she was quiet. "Etta, there is nothing wrong with wanting pleasure for yourself. With seeking it in a place like this or somewhere else."

"I hope not, because I'm here now. And I have no idea what to do."

"I could introduce you to a few gentlemen. Or ladies, if you prefer."

Bernadette's eyes widened. "I hadn't thought of ladies. What a concept! But no, I think it is a gentleman who would fit the bill.

But…" She hesitated. "May I wait to take that generous offer? Perhaps tonight I could just…look. Watch. And get up my nerve."

"Certainly." Annabelle squeezed her hand again. "Do as you like. Here you have all the freedom in the world to do so. And I'm just across the room if you change your mind, or if you become overwhelmed. Good evening."

Bernadette smiled at her, kind all over again. "Thank you."

Annabelle slipped away, and Bernadette drew a long breath as she looked again at the people around her. A lady she thought for certain she recognized as a normally staid countess was being propped up on a table by not one but two men, and if the kissing and touching was any indication, it was all about to get even more arousing.

But before she could decide if she was going to watch or flee, she felt a hand curl around her upper arm and she pivoted to find a man towering over her. Only it wasn't just any man. Masked or not, she knew it was Theo even before he spoke. And judging from the thin line of his mouth and the fire in his gaze, he seemed to know it was her, too.

A guess that was proven true when he hissed, "What the hell are you doing here?"

It wasn't fair of Theo not to give Etta a chance to answer his question. He knew that. But people were watching and likely listening and so instead of waiting for her to speak, he was now guiding her across the room toward the back hallway where the private suites were guarded.

To his surprise, she didn't argue or fight back against his heavy-handed behavior. She simply scurried to keep up with him as she sent him side glances past the edge of her pearl mask.

"A room," Theo snapped, flashing a pin on his lapel that indicated the level of his membership.

"Of course." The large man guarding the hall glanced at his sheet. "Room twelve is open. It isn't a viewing room."

"Perfect," Theo grunted, and they entered the dim hallway and headed toward the end.

"I—" she began.

He held up a hand and opened the door, rushing her in. He turned the key, which didn't actually lock the door, but indicated the room was in use. Then he faced her and tore his mask off.

"I am going to repeat my question, only with cursing because I cannot be expected to meter my language under these circumstances. What the fuck are you doing here, Bernadette?"

"How did you know it was me?" she asked, and lifted shaking hands to lower her own mask.

His breath caught as she dropped it onto the big bed beside her. Somehow the fact that they had both removed their masks made him feel naked and now they stared at each other in the quiet of the room. Well, not entirely quiet. He could hear a woman moaning in the distance, from one of the other rooms.

Apparently Etta could hear it too because she blushed and her gaze fluttered away from his. "Theo," she said softly, her voice catching a little. "I was wearing an old dress I doubt you'd remember and my hair is done a bit more...wildly?"

Theo let his gaze flit over said hair. She was right in the use of wild. She had it all tumbled atop her head, soft and a little untamed and definitely taunting a man's fingers to drag it all down.

She continued, "And I was wearing a mask. But if you could recognize me, I need to know how so that I can keep anyone else from doing the same when I'm here."

He shut his eyes briefly. So she didn't intend this little visit to be a one-time thing. And her question was a valid one. The answer would reveal too much to her, as it did to himself, but there was no avoiding it.

"I've known you so long, Etta, that I know you the moment you walk into any room. Back turned to me, dimly lit, with a mask and in a dress I don't recall, I would know it was you, no matter what. I looked across that crowded room where all those people were writhing together and I knew you." Her breath caught, her pupils dilated and her gaze briefly rolled over his entire body before she returned it to his face at last. He shook his head, trying to break this spell he didn't want to fall under. "But that isn't the point."

She tilted her head. "What is the point, Theo?"

He let out a long, ragged sigh. "This is the *third* time I'm asking this and I'm rapidly running out of patience. Why are you here?"

Her nostrils flared slightly and her shoulders trembled when she whispered, "I told you what I wanted yesterday. And you made it abundantly clear that you didn't have advice or…or anything else for me. You turned away."

"So you ran *here?*" he asked, hating himself for creating a scenario where she might have endangered herself.

"You keep acting like this is some terrible place," she said. "But it has rules, there are other ladies here, and if you didn't follow me here, then you must have your own membership. I doubt you would keep that if you thought women were being harmed in these walls."

He frowned. She had a point there. The Donville Masquerade was a good establishment, despite the shocking freedom of its gatherings. Marcus Rivers had an unshakable moral compass and took care of any villain who might get past the gate with swift efficiency. So maybe Theo's hesitation wasn't about safety after all.

And he hated acknowledging that to himself.

He stared at her, with her cheeks flaming with embarrassment. Perhaps she didn't fully understand, even if he had caught her in the hall watching with rapt attention to what was happening around her. But she was innocent, even if she had been married, so perhaps she needed a better education. To really understand what she was getting herself into here.

"You have this fantasy," he said, moving toward her in a few long strides across the small room.

She backed up but he allowed her no quarter, looming over her as she crashed back against the edge of the bed. She reached a hand back to steady herself, and when her fingers sank into the plush coverlet, clenching into a fist around the fabric, his heart began to pound so hard it was difficult to hear anything else but its rushing in his ears.

He forced himself to continue, "This vague desire for the passion you see between your friends and their husbands. It's all very romantic and gauzy and vague." He leaned in, letting himself breathe in the scent of her without pressing his mouth to her throat. "But this place isn't romantic, Etta. It's a place for lovers." He leaned back. "For *fucking*."

He expected her to turn away, to blush further, to push him even, because he was being very ungentlemanly now. But instead she reached a hand up and pressed it to his chest, her fingers fluttering there against his body as she closed whatever sliver of distance remained between them.

"Well..." she whispered, her voice shaking. "I...I want to be...fucked."

Watching her lips form that word, feeling her touch him as she did so, it was too much. He caught her around the waist, molding her to him and his mouth came down hard on hers, claiming her kiss once more.

The first time Theo kissed her it had been gentle. Oh, it had awakened things in her, certainly, but he hadn't driven her too hard or fast. But this...this kiss was something else. He was animal and he devoured her, moaning against her lips as he invaded every part of her mouth. And she welcomed him, meeting his kiss with hunger that had been loosened when she watched those wicked things in the room outside that door. Hunger set completely free the moment this man touched her.

Perhaps he was trying to frighten her, as he had been trying to do when he hauled her into this room, when he used such harsh language with her, when he tried to scoot her away from what she wanted. But none of it worked. The more blunt he was, the more she wanted him. And the harder he pushed her now, the more it woke a part of her she wanted to explore.

A part that didn't follow rules or watch from the sidelines or live in fear.

So when he crowded her against the bed and she tumbled onto her back, she didn't feel panic. She felt a thrill of excitement and a pulse of sensation that seemed to make every nerve ending in her body tingle. Especially the ones between her legs, a place where only *she* had been able to stimulate a response in her life.

"Tell me to stop," he whispered as he continued to rise up over her at the edge of the bed, the firelight behind him putting him in darkness.

But she wasn't afraid of the dark. "I don't want you to stop," she managed to croak out.

He bent his head, almost as if he were defeated, and then he leaned over, caught her behind the knees and tugged her to the edge of the mattress so her legs dangled off the side and her bottom was almost sliding off entirely.

"If that changes, you need to tell me," he said, his voice shaking.

And then he shocked her by beginning to hitch her skirt up her legs.

CHAPTER 5

If Bernadette was honest with herself, and in this moment she could be nothing but honest, she had pictured being touched by Theo more than once. She dreamed of him kissing her every so often, even when she was just a girl.

More recently, in those moments when she gave herself pleasure with her hand, sometimes it was *his* face that invaded her vague erotic fantasies.

But the reality of him was not the same. She sat up on her elbows, watching him, taking in every moment as he leaned over her. His hands were warm as they glided beneath the edge of her skirt. He pushed it up and up her body. His thumbs circled her kneecaps, he gripped tighter as he reached her thighs, where her stockings where tied and met the edge of her drawers.

"Tsk, tsk," he murmured without looking up at her face. "If you come to the Donville Masquerade, you can't wear these." Now he did look at her as he caught the edge of the fabric right where the drawers split and then rent them in half with what seemed like no effort. He tugged the frayed pieces of soft cotton away and then turned aside to toss them in the fire where they all but disintegrated in a flame that lifted the light in the room for a fraction of a moment.

Bernadette's face blazed just as hot when he turned back and looked at her again, this time without anything covering her, protecting her from his gaze between her legs.

"There is so much consternation created about this," Theo said softly, and pressed hand to each of her bare thighs, spreading her open wider, stepping into the space between her legs. "About you protecting yourself from…" He let his thumb trace the crease there and she arched up with a gasp. "…plunderers. Of virginity somehow being king, even once it's physically no longer an issue. But what you say you want from some man…from me…defies all that." He looked at her. "Still want to say yes?"

She nodded. "Y-Yes."

If he was trying to goad her into backing away, he certainly looked pleased when she voiced her consent to continue. Almost relieved. He began to massage her outer lips with his thumbs and she jolted at the electric pleasure it created. When he peeled her open, she turned her head and he stopped moving.

"Watch," he ordered. "If this is what you want, then be here, Etta. Be here in this moment."

She drew in a ragged breath and did as he said. She looked at him again and watched as he slowly lowered his head toward her now fully exposed sex. She gripped the coverlet, uncertain as to what he was doing. But then his mouth found her and she gasped at the pure sensation of his tongue tracing her entrance.

"Theo," she gasped, gliding one hand into his hair.

He chuckled against her body and the vibrations made her twist and moan even more. She was on fire, she was alive and it felt even better than she'd built it up to be in her mind. She ground up into him as his tongue found her clitoris, circling her lightly. Too lightly. He was teasing her, tormenting her. She wasn't sure if she wanted it to end or last forever.

She didn't seem to have much choice in the matter. He licked her length again and then returned to her clitoris, but this time with more firm intention. He increased the pressure of his mouth, dragging his tongue over the sensitive nub over and over again. What she'd felt as she drove herself to orgasm paled in comparison to this, and she jerked against him, losing herself.

She felt his fingers still moving even as his tongue drove against her. He spread her open farther, allowing his tongue more access. And then he breached her, gently and slowly, with one finger. She hadn't been taken since before her husband's death, and the feel of Theo's body entering her, even in this small way, increased her pleasure even more. She gripped him, arching her hips, seeking her pleasure. When he added a second finger, she lost control. He pumped into her, gently even as he sucked and licked her with abandon.

The pleasure built, growing immense and undeniable and wild. She surrendered to it and to him, riding the waves of sensation as they got bigger and bigger. The end was coming, release was near, but she trusted him to take her there. When he did, the explosion was something unlike anything she'd ever felt before.

Pleasure overtook her and she rose into it, crying out like she'd heard others in the rooms around her cry out. She gasped and moaned and her body jerked out of control, but Theo kept up, never breaking contact, never slowing the pump of his fingers as she gripped around him in wave after wave of release. Only when she collapsed back, her aching body letting go, did he stop, sucking her once more before he kissed her hip, her thigh.

He moved up her body, joining her on the bed. He kissed her mouth and she tasted her pleasure on his lips. Salty and sweet, earthy and powerful. She pulled him in closer, weak and warm and ready for whatever would come next.

Only it didn't. He gentled his kisses instead of increasing them and finally pulled away to look down at her. His expression was unreadable in the dim quiet. Aroused, yes. But not driven. Her heart sank.

"Bernadette," he whispered.

She flinched. He wouldn't even use the name that had become his term of endearment. "Please," she whispered, whimpered and she hated herself for it.

He shook his head. "Let me take you home."

"I don't want to go home," she said, and pushed him away to sit up.

He let her go, watching her from his position sprawled on the big bed. His hair was mussed from her grip and his lips were shining from her pleasure. He looked so wicked and yet he refused, over and over, to be fully wicked with *her*.

She saw him grit his teeth, saw his frustration with her. But also saw his desire. Good, if she was going to be frustrated, she wanted him to be too. He deserved it.

"Emotions are high," he said softly. "And in those moments, bad decisions can be made."

She stared at him. Was he talking about himself? About what they had just shared in that bed where he still lay, looking like a king who had plundered a land he didn't even want now. It took all the air out of her in that moment. He'd been right on the edge of surrender, of pleasure, of passion and he could just…stop. It wasn't good for the ego. And he wasn't wrong that in this state, she could easily make a mistake.

"Please let me take you home," he repeated, this time gentler.

She let out her breath in a harsh sigh and grabbed her mask, sliding it back over her face. "Fine. Have it your way."

She didn't wait for his response, she just smoothed her hands over her skirt to make sure she was back in place and then headed for the door. But she had no idea how she would ever regroup after this deeply pleasurable and somehow catastrophic night.

She just hoped it wouldn't be her only chance to feel the high he had gifted her just before he dashed her on the rocks once again.

∼

Theo sat across from Bernadette in her carriage, watching her in the dim light. She was angry, that much was clear from the way she folded her arms across her chest and refused to look at him except to occasionally glare in his general direction. The anger he could have dealt with, truth be told.

It was the fact that under the anger, he could feel her hurt that struck him mute and made his hands shake. That and the fact that he could still taste her on his tongue, still feel the clench of her against his fingers.

He had to get himself together so he could figure out what to do next. Especially since the carriage was pulling into the drive and came to a stop in front of her home on Kent's Row. Servants began to appear from the stable, but she held up a hand at the window and they all stepped back.

Once again, she looked at him, but the heat was gone from her gaze. She sighed. "I know you think I'm...I'm foolish. Stupid even."

He sat up straighter at that. "*Never!*"

"Don't lie to me. You're playing some game, trying to trick me out of what I want because...I can't even imagine why. I assume some misguided sense of protection because you think I'm made of glass and incapable of deciding to do anything on my own."

She shook her head and once again he felt the pain beneath the surface of all this. He couldn't help but think about her all those years ago, when they'd stood together in a gazebo and she'd reminded him that she would never have freedom. That she would always be under some man's thumb. He had made sure she would be, hadn't he? By refusing her then, even though she didn't know that he had done it.

Perhaps by refusing her now.

"You're not alone in that," she continued. "My father felt the same way, My husband did, as well. You are another in a long line of men who would deny me what I feel. And now you've brought me home, done your duty. So good night, Your Grace."

She pivoted to leave, but he caught her arm and held her there. "No. Not like this. We're not finished."

He flinched when he heard those words from his own mouth. Why had he said them? She'd given him the perfect out, the perfect way to cut this off. He could have apologized, released her, sent her some sad flowers later and let it be. She might not even go to the Donville Masquerade again if he'd somehow ruined that place for her.

But he didn't *want* to ruin things. He didn't want to hurt her to make his point or guide her actions.

"No?" she said, shaking his hand away. "You want to finish now like you wouldn't back in the hell?"

He clenched his jaw at the taunt. She had no idea how close he'd been to doing exactly what she'd wanted. To losing control. To forgetting himself and her and just taking what he wanted.

"I want to *talk* to you," he managed to grind out.

She laughed, though there was no humor to the sound. "Wonderful. More talk. Talk, talk, talk." She pushed open the door. "The duke will be joining me," she called up to her butler. "He wants to *talk*."

She left him behind in the carriage as she strode into the house with every male servant staring after her in slack-jawed awe. Theo couldn't blame them. There was something in the fire of her anger that made him want to...stoke it. To make her hotter and sharper and more and more passionate, whether it was in his bed or any other place.

He blinked to clear that thought and slowly followed her into the house and down the hall into her parlor. She had crossed to the sideboard ahead of him and sloshed bourbon into two glasses, one of which she waved vaguely toward him without actually taking the other herself.

"So talk," she snapped, and paced away.

"Etta," he said gently.

She pivoted back. "Don't call me that."

The order stung and Theo found himself stepping back from her as if he could avoid a dagger flung at his chest. "Wh-why?" he asked.

"Because it doesn't belong to you," she gasped out, and there was the pain again, pulsing beneath the anger. "You do it and you try to make it special. Pretend that *I'm* special to you, but I'm not."

"That's not true," he began, despite how dangerous those words were.

She threw up her hands. "How? The truth of it is, we knew each other as children when we were pushed together by the circumstance of the friendship of our wretched fathers. You didn't choose my company. And then you didn't speak to me beyond a bored *good day* until Valaria came to the Row and you were forced back into my sphere by the feelings of your best friend. None of what you do, how you talk to me, what you say to me means *anything*."

That accusation tore through him, and in that moment he recognized the absolute lie of it. It was terrifying to feel the truth and he should have left. But somehow he couldn't. He couldn't walk away like this and destroy whatever was being built between them.

He did step toward her then. "I would hope that what just happened between us in that room in the hell shows you that whatever I do, it means *something*."

He saw those words move through her, shock her, tempt her, but then she hardened herself to them, to him. She shrugged. "If gossip is to be believed, you do that and far more with many women."

She wasn't wrong. His reputation had been born from truth, even if he hadn't cultivated it on the same level in the last year or so. Why he'd stopped playing so much...well, that was not something he wished to consider. There was too much to this situation to do so. Once again, he was being left with a chance to walk away. To keep himself from wading into waters with this woman that felt too deep, too dangerous.

Only he didn't. He drew a deep breath and shook his head. "Not like what just happened with you, Etta. It's never been like it just was with you."

CHAPTER 6

Bernadette stared at Theo, uncertain if she was dreaming…or if she'd simply taken his meaning wrong. But he was looking at her so evenly, so certainly…

"You—you don't mean that," she whispered.

A shadow of a smile worked over his handsome face. "You have an awful lot of opinions about my feelings. But you aren't inside of my head. So let me disabuse you of some misconceptions."

Bernadette shifted. "Fine."

"You didn't mean nothing to me when we were children. I considered us friends of a sort." He ticked one finger off his hand, but then his expression grew a bit troubled. "I-I know you remember that day in the gazebo."

She stiffened because she often thought of that day so long ago when she and Theo had connected over their lack of control over their lives. "Yes."

He leaned a little closer. "Do you think I admitted my struggles to everyone the way I did with you that day?"

There was a flash of vulnerability that crossed his face, just as it had that long ago day. Something he *chose* to show her, it seemed, even though she could see how uncomfortable it made him. "No," she said softly. "If you say you didn't, then I believe you."

"Then I hope you'll also believe that when I call you Etta, it's because I always felt it suited you."

"How did you hear it?" she asked, blinking back tears. "Only my grandfather ever called me that."

He shifted. "I met him once, just before his death. He was your mother's father, yes?"

She nodded and a flood of thoughts about the man rushed through her. His kind smile, his gentleness, the way he'd sneaked her sweets.

"My father mentioned he was friends with yours and he lit up. He turned to me and said that I must know his Etta. I never thought of you as anything else ever again. But if you don't like me to call you that, *Bernadette*, I won't."

She drew in a long breath and turned away from him, pacing across the room to the fire. She placed a hand on the mantel, steadying herself as she stared into the flames. "He was the only person who…" She choked on the words and struggled to continue. "Who cared about me. And that little name made me feel special."

"Because you are."

She faced him to determine if he was saying that with pity or with something else. But he was too hard to read now. He no longer showed the truth of himself. But by God, he was handsome as he stood there across that small room, his attention focused entirely on her.

"I do like it when you use it," she said. "He's been gone so long that it's become *your* nickname for me, no longer his. All that's left is that feeling. But you should also know that it's the secret name I gave at the Donville Masquerade. For my membership."

His brows lifted. "I see. Well, I'll be careful in how I use it then."

"You followed me in here demanding we talk," she said. "Is there anything else?"

"Yes, the most important topic of all," he said, and he moved toward her again.

The way he closed the distance between them, his eyes locked on hers, brought her to mind of how he'd crowded her into the bed at the club and she shivered with anticipation she ought not have. Not when he kept walking away from her just as easily.

"What is that?" she asked, and wished her hands weren't shaking.

"You say that I don't want you," he said. "But I do." Her breath caught, but he didn't allow her to interrupt. "I wanted you when we kissed yesterday. I wanted you at the Donville Masquerade." He hesitated and cleared his throat. "And I...I want you now, Etta."

Her heart was beating so loudly now that she was sure he could hear it as he loomed over her, too close and somehow still too far away. He was offering her something and yet she didn't fully believe it based on what had happened between them recently.

"Then why did you run away after we kissed?" she asked. "Why didn't you have me in that back room in the hell?"

She saw him struggle with the answer, shifting and moving, his hands smoothing along the front of his jacket. But at last he said, "Because I don't want to hurt you. I never want to hurt you."

It felt like a lifetime that Etta just stared at him, but at last her expression softened. She closed the little space he'd left between them and gently took his hand. As her fingers threaded through his own, he shivered. It was such a simple touch, and yet it moved him so much. More than he should allow.

"You aren't going to hurt me, Theo," she said, staring up into his face with those beautiful dark eyes. "I know ladies often tie what I'm asking for to their hearts, to their futures, but I have none of those expectations."

Those words should have comforted him. They were exactly what men claimed to want to hear from women. She was talking about sin, passion…sex, with no strings attached. No demands. And yet he felt a little hollow when she said them.

"Then what do you want?" he asked to fill the space, to forget that it existed.

"I want to feel what I felt in that room. I want to drown in it." She lifted his hand and settled it against her heart. "I felt so over my head at the club, Theo. I'll go back if I must, but with you it feels… safe. I'd rather be with my friend, with you, if you'd help me."

Theo let his eyes come shut and he let out a ragged breath. He'd been trying to fight this desire for this woman for even longer than he wished he admit. It had only been harder since she declared she wished for a lover and then made it clear she would find one with or without him.

He wasn't going to be able to resist her anymore. Not now that he knew her taste, that he had felt the grip of her when she came. Not now when she was offering so much and asking for so little. Not now when what she offered was everything. He was too weak to keep walking away. He hoped he could still be strong enough to protect her…protect himself…in other ways.

Because this was going to shift his world. There was no getting around it.

He tugged her a little closer and wrapped his arms around her. She fit so perfectly against him that it set him off kilter and he had to adjust his stance to keep from staggering.

"I'm going to take you upstairs, Etta," he said, his voice rough to his own ears. "I'm going to take off your dress and I'm going to make what happened in the hell look like something to whet the appetite, nothing more."

Her eyes went wide. "O-oh."

He nodded. "I'm going to take you if that's what you want. And then, tomorrow, when everything feels less…sharp, you and I will have a long talk about terms and what will happen next. But for now…"

He shivered as he bent his head. She met him halfway and they kissed. And just like every other time that had happened, he was set back on his heels. He held her closer, reveling in the taste of her, in her increasing daring as her tongue tangled with his. Of the soft sound of pleasure she made. He wanted to make her do that more and more. He wanted her weak with pleasure, drunk on him. He wanted to be drunk on her. And now that he'd accepted that was the undeniable path of their future, he wanted it to start immediately.

So he drew back, looking down into her desire-filled face and said, "Now take me to your room, Etta. Let's begin."

~

Bernadette's hands shook as she led Theo through the doors to her chamber. It was a nice room, with a pretty view of the garden behind the house. Her fire glowed and the bedclothes were already turned back on one side, she supposed in anticipation of her lonely return from wherever her maid thought she'd been that night.

"You look nervous," he said with a smile as he shut the door, then locked it with a click of the key, which sounded like a gunshot to her sensitive system.

She caught her breath. She had to speak. She couldn't just stare at him like a ninny.

"I am," she admitted. "I'm realizing that no man has ever been in this room, beyond whatever servants moved my things in upon my arrival almost five years ago."

His eyes lit up. "So I'm an explorer," he said with a laugh that eased her worries a little. "I promise I won't move the furniture around."

She feared he would move far more than the furniture but kept that thought to herself. It was too dangerous to consider, let alone speak, when she'd just given such a big speech downstairs about how she had no expectations about whatever would happen between them physically.

"Etta," he said softly, and she jolted as she brought her focus back on him. "What do you want to feel like?"

She stared at him, not understanding the question. "I…what do you mean?"

He moved toward her. "I'm going to touch you. How I touch you will make you feel things. If you tell me what you want to feel, I can best give you that."

"How I want to feel?" she repeated in confusion, trying to picture how Tunbridge had touched her all those years ago. She doubted he'd ever thought once about what she felt when he did.

Theo's brow wrinkled, almost like he was a little concerned that she so obviously didn't understand his meaning. Was this what everyone did and she was just a little fool for not knowing?

He traced a fingertip along her jawline and she shivered at the sensation of his touch. God, how could he do that with something so simple?

"You could want to feel safe," he whispered as he turned her around so her back was to him. She felt the softness of his breath against the nape of her neck and leaned against his chest with a shiver. He rumbled a little, deep in his chest when she did so and the room felt like it had begun to spin.

"Or perhaps you want to feel devoured," he continued, and unfastened one of the buttons along the back of her dress. "Over-powered. Dominated so that you can surrender."

She heard a moan escape her lips at that thought, but she couldn't make herself speak.

"You might want to be teased," he continued, and unfastened another button, then another. "A little erotic torture where you're begging for release."

"Theo," she whispered.

"Or maybe you want to be worshipped," he said unbuttoning the last two fastenings at the back of her dress. His hands slid beneath the fabric, gliding along her ribcage through her silky chemise beneath. "Like you're the only woman in the world."

She looked over her shoulder at him and nodded. "That. I want that. I want to feel desired unlike any woman you've ever been with. Even if I know that's a lie. Make me believe it."

He held her gaze for what felt like an eternity and then he nodded. He turned her to face him again and slowly slid his fingers into her hair. He tilted her head gently, lifting her mouth toward his, and then he kissed her.

There was something different about this kiss. She felt it the moment his lips met hers. Perhaps because they'd already gone so far, or because they'd discussed such intimate things…or perhaps it was because there would be no more running or hiding or avoiding what was about to come. He kissed her and it was a claiming, a coming home. A connection that made her knees shake.

"You are so beautiful," he murmured against her lips as he drew her gown down off her shoulders and around her waist. He hooked his thumbs beneath the fabric and pushed over her hips so that the silk pooled at her feet. This left her in only her chemise. He had torn her drawers off earlier and the edge of the chemise barely skimmed her thighs. She felt revealed, exposed.

Even more so when he stepped back and looked at her in the flickering firelight. "God, so beautiful. You've always been so beautiful and I—" He cut himself off, and this time he almost sounded pained. "It will be easy to worship you—you *should* be worshipped."

He reached out a hand and settled it on her shoulder, fingers playing with the thin strap of her chemise. The brush of his fingertips against her bare skin was unlike anything she'd ever felt before. It made her feel alive and tingly and needy. She whimpered softly without even meaning to.

That sound made his dark blue eyes go wide and his smile grew wicked. But he didn't say anything, he just stepped up to her, closing the slender distance between them. He wrapped an arm around her waist, but he didn't hold her. Instead he gripped the fabric of her chemise into a fist against her back. It forced the hem of the garment to lift, exposing her further.

But he wasn't looking at her body, he was staring into her eyes. And there it was, the exact feeling she had asked for a few moments before. He was so entirely focused on her, she *did* feel like the only woman in the world. Like he valued her above everything else. It was so bewitching. She wanted to sink into it, but also knew she needed to recall this was a game.

"How long has it been since you were naked with a man?" he whispered, cupping her cheek, stroking his fingers across her lips gently.

Her breath was so ragged she almost couldn't speak. "Since before Tunbridge's death." She saw his brow wrinkle, but then the confusion was gone. He was seductive and sure again.

"Then I'm honored to be the first in a long time." He slid a finger beneath the chemise strap. "May I?"

She nodded, though she wasn't actually certain she was ready to be perceived in such a vulnerable way. But that was why she'd chosen Theo, wasn't it? That was why she trusted him with this moment. So she surrendered to it, surrendered to him, and knew deep in her soul that what happened next was going to be magnificent.

CHAPTER 7

Theo had been with a great many women, just as Etta had accused him of earlier in the night. He liked sex, he liked giving and receiving pleasure. He never let the needs of his body get tangled up in the feelings of his heart, and everyone left satisfied.

But right now, as he lowered Etta's chemise strap, his hands shook. That was no act to show her that she was worshipped—it was his true reaction to touching her, to knowing what she was about to share with him. That was a heady thing and his head spun with it.

He leaned in, breathing in the scent of her. A musky vanilla that had been haunting him for far longer than the last few days of sudden and irrevocable desire. He could lose himself in it.

She made a soft sound as she turned her face toward his. Their lips were almost touching but he didn't push for another kiss. Instead, he slowly drew the strap down her arm until it bowed at her elbow. Then he did the same with the other and let the fabric fall over her breasts.

He looked at her and caught his breath. She was so very lovely exposed like this. Her breasts were not too heavy for her slender frame and her nipples were a dark rose. He left her chemise caught around her ribcage and stroked the back of his hand back up and over her right breast to cup its weight in his hand. He stroked a thumb over her already hard nipple and she dipped her head back with a hiss.

She was so sensitive and it lit him on fire because he knew he could access her pleasure in so many ways. Giving pleasure had always aroused him, but all those other times paled in comparison to this. To her.

He bent his head and lightly traced the shape of her nipple with the tip of his tongue. Her fingers dug into his hair and she cried out in the quiet. He smiled against her flesh and held her closer, sucking now, licking as she writhed against him and made soft mewls and groans. He shifted to the other nipple and repeated the pleasure there, watching up the line of her body as she arched. Her head was thrown back, her eyes squeezed shut, her lips slightly parted with pleasure.

He wanted to give more and more of that. Until she shattered like she had against his tongue. Until she shuttered around him, milking his own pleasure with hers.

He shoved her chemise down the rest of her body as he traced his mouth up over her breast and back to the hollow of her throat. "Lie down on the bed," he whispered against her wild pulse.

She drew back. "I don't want you to stop."

He heard the desperation in her voice, felt it in the way she trembled, and hesitated. He'd caused those reactions, of course, by denying her earlier. But there was more to this than just him. He felt it, knew it. And he wanted to ease it, soothe it, despite the fact that it wasn't his place. It could never be his place.

"I'm not going to stop," he assured her instead.

She held his gaze and her relief was as palpable as her desire. She nodded wordlessly and then stepped from his arms and to the bed. As she settled into a place on the pillows, covering herself with her hands, he went to work on his own clothing.

She watched him as he shed his jacket and his waistcoat. As he unwound his cravat and unbuttoned his shirt. When he tugged it over his head and tossed it over his shoulder, she sat up with a sharp intake of breath.

He smiled and tried not to preen. But it was almost impossible when she was looking at him like that. "Like what you see, Your Grace?"

She nodded. "Very much so, Your Grace."

He laughed at her repeat of their titles and stepped toward the bed so she could look more closely. "Examine away," he murmured.

She scooted closer and reached out a hand, tracing her fingers across his pectoral muscle and then down the midline of his chest. The touch was so delicate, but it lit him on fire like nothing he'd experienced for a very long time. She followed the line of chest hair that disappeared into his trouser-waist, drawing a fingertip along the edge of the fabric there with a shiver.

She looked up at him then. "When you touch me, even just in the gentlest way, it does something to me. It makes me feel...feel wobbly. Tingly. Alive. Does it do the same for you when I touch you?"

He nodded. "Yes." She continued to play along the waist of his trousers and he sucked in a breath. "Like what you're doing just there. Fire."

She wrinkled her brow and dragged her hand back and forth in the same place. "This?"

"Yes." His tone was garbled.

She pulled her hand away and he was as disappointed as he was released from her intoxicating spell. She swallowed hard. "May I see the rest?"

Theo blinked, not at the question but at the reaction in his body. He'd never been self-conscious about his nudity before, but he felt... nervous. How was that possible?

He pushed the sensation aside and stepped back to slowly unfasten the fall front of his trousers. He lowered the flap and caught himself in hand, stroking the half-hard length of himself and barely holding back a groan. He was so sensitive at present that he feared he wouldn't last long if he wasn't careful.

And he wanted to last a very long time for her.

Her breath went from short to nonexistent and she stared at him, eyes a little glazed. "I...I don't know if that will fit."

He glanced down at the hard length of his cock and shook his head. He was of average size, not enormous. He might have expected such a comment if she were a virgin, but not from someone who had been with another man in her life.

"You and Tunbridge did have relations, didn't you?" he asked.

She nodded. "We did. But I didn't see..." She waved her hand at his cock.

He stared at her. "He never let you see him?"

Now redness entered her cheeks and she flopped back against the bed and covered her head with a pillow. "I sound ridiculous. Oh, I knew I would ruin this somehow and—"

"It's not ruined, far from ruined," he interrupted, shoving his trousers off so he wouldn't trip over them and sitting down on the edge of the bed next to her. "Etta, will you please look at me?"

She took a moment before she lifted the pillow and peeked out at him. "I'm sorry."

He shook his head. "If that was how he made love to you, that's his failing, not yours, my dear. Did you like it when he bedded you?"

Her long silence was his answer and he briefly despised the late Duke of Tunbridge. "I see. Well, all the more reason to fully worship you, as you were meant to be worshipped. But first, sit up."

She did so slowly, her cheeks still bright with embarrassed color.

"Will you please touch me?" he asked.

She stared at his length once more and then timidly reached out to trace her finger along him. He couldn't hold back a little moan of pleasure. Fuck, but he wanted her. He fought to focus so he could make this perfect for her.

"I promise you this won't hurt you," he said. "Do you trust me?"

Now her gaze came up to his face and he realized that he had just asked a very loaded question. Her answer would be about more than pleasure and sex, it would be about their friendship, their relationship going forward, however they defined it once they had spent this night together.

Her answer was about him.

"Yes," she said at last, the word barely carrying. "I trust you, Theo."

Those words meant too much and he ignored the swell of emotion in his heart when she said them.

"Good." He slid his fingers into her hair, combing through the locks so they fell around her shoulders. "Then just let me sweep you away. If you don't like what I do, you'll tell me and I'll fix it. I promise."

She was quiet a long moment, and then she said, "Theo?"

"Yes?"

"I feel desired. I feel worshipped." She leaned in. "And I want you to continue."

She kissed him, wrapping her arms around his neck. He leaned into her, lowering her back on the pillows, shifting to partially cover her with his body. The feel of her skin on his skin was magic and he arched into her, needing more, needing everything. She responded, lifting against him, her mouth growing hungrier, her tongue seeking harder.

"Please," she whimpered between kisses.

It nearly unmanned him there and then. It nearly pushed him to take and claim as his body was screaming at him to do. But he had made a promise to her. And he intended to keep it.

So he glided his mouth from hers and began.

B ernadette wasn't certain what she had expected once she and Theo were naked. A quick claiming, she supposed, hopefully filled with more of the sensation he inspired in her. But what he was doing now, tracing the lines of her body with his tongue as his hands roved over her, it was something more than she'd ever known she wanted.

He lit her on fire and she was lost, sinking into sensation, releasing everything else that held her back. She would surrender now, let him have his way with her because she had told him she trusted him, and she did. Potentially to her own detriment, but still true.

He was sucking her nipple again, his big hand resting lightly on her stomach, stroking the flesh there that she had never known was so sensitive. It felt like her entire being was throbbing, pulsing in time to his touch. And all the sensation was starting to settle in one place: right between her legs.

As if he sensed that, he slid his hand lower, caressing her hip and then pressing his fingers into her thigh. She opened her legs out of instinct and he made a soft sound against her breast even as his tongue swirled faster and harder around her nipple.

When he stroked his fingers across her entrance, she could feel how wet she was. There was no resistance, only pleasure, and she lifted into him, wanting his fingers inside of her again as they had been when he licked her so intimately in the club what felt like hours and hours and hours ago.

But he didn't claim this time. He stroked her, opening her, teasing her, swirling a fingertip around her clitoris and reminding her how good that place could feel. She lifted into him, grinding for pleasure almost against her will. He let her, lifting his head from her body, watching her intently as she gasped and moaned in time to his teasing.

"Please," she gasped again, not caring that she was begging him. She just needed…well, she couldn't really name what she needed. But it was far more than his mouth or his fingers could provide.

His gaze grew almost feral in that moment, heated and even more focused on her, which shocked her. She didn't think he could be more in tune with her needs than he already was.

"Yes," he murmured, and moved to his knees over her.

He pushed between her legs, widening her, opening her fully. He continued to massage her sex, stroking her clitoris with ever more firm strokes. She felt the edge of release coming, just as it had earlier, and she reached for it, gripping the coverlet with both hands, breath short, body twisting almost against her will.

And then she came, long waves of pleasure moving through her body. In that moment, he pressed his cock to her and slid inside in one thrust. He definitely fit, and without any trouble, only pleasure. She whimpered out his name as he covered her, digging her nails into his back as he began to thrust, grinding his pelvis against her with every stroke. She gripped him as her orgasm continued, her body going wild.

He kissed her, increasing his thrusts, rolling her through the pleasure, lengthening it even as he moaned his own desire. She wanted him to find it, she wanted to give him the same release he was giving her. She wanted to feel him lose control and know that it was her who had inspired it, even for just a moment.

He lifted his head and their eyes locked. She lifted into him, clenching with more purpose as the veins in his neck pulsed. "Fuck," he grunted.

She nodded. "Please," she said yet again, this time begging for something else.

He pushed harder, digging his fingers into her thigh as he drew her leg up higher against his hip. He hit differently then, some place deep inside of her that was powerful. Then he gasped and suddenly withdrew, the heat of him pumping against his hand, splashing on her skin as he came. And he was beautiful in it, his jaw clenched, his eyes squeezed shut, his head thrown back as he spent.

Then he collapsed over her, kissing her all over again, bringing her down from the pleasure as surely as he had drawn her up to it. She was weightless in his arms, clinging to him for purchase. And she realized as they lay there that whatever she had expected or imagined or fantasized about, this man was more than she ever could have dreamed.

Which made the potential for pain when this was over far higher than she'd told herself it could be. So she had to be careful and remember this was nothing more than an affair. It couldn't be anything else.

CHAPTER 8

Theo should have felt good after the hours he'd spent in Etta's bed. And he did. How could he not when what had happened between them was so powerful, so pleasurable? But he also felt… discombobulated. Out of sorts. Restless. And he hated to admit why.

He'd slipped away at dawn, hours before, leaving just a note on the pillow beside her, telling her to come to him at eleven so they could talk about the future of…well, whatever this was. Now he found himself watching the clock, waiting with an anxiety unlike anything he'd ever felt before.

"Bollocks," he muttered, pacing across his study once more.

"Your Grace?" Kimball said at the door.

Theo pivoted toward the butler. "Yes?"

Was that a croak to his tone? Jesus, he was out of control.

"You have a guest," Kimball said, and relief and excitement immediately flooded Theo's entire body. "The Duke of Blackvale." Theo felt his expression fall at the mention of his best friend's name and he saw confusion flutter on his butler's face. "Your Grace?"

"Of course," Theo grunted, trying desperately to get himself back together. "Send Callum in."

Kimball still looked confused as he exited the room, and Theo realized he only had a few moments to gather himself. Callum knew him too well for him to act like this. He would ask questions, he would press, and Theo had no intention to talk about what had happened with Etta. Callum would read too much into it.

He smoothed his jacket as Callum entered the room, grin on his face and hand outstretched. "Theo..." He stopped mid-stride and stared at him. "What is it?"

"Fucking hell," Theo muttered, and turned away. "I'm fine. What are you doing here?"

Now Callum leaned back. "Well, you've been distracted since the wedding and I'm leaving with Valaria tomorrow morning, so I thought I'd take the opportunity to say goodbye to you."

"Of course." Theo shook his head. He'd entirely forgotten. "Of course, my apologies."

"Why do you look terrible?" Callum asked, taking a seat before Theo's fire and folding his arms.

"Oh yes, please sit," Theo said, turning to the veil of sarcasm to keep Callum from the heart of the matter. "Make yourself at home. May I get you a drink?"

"I *have* made myself at home, and it's half past ten. I'm not drinking at half past ten." Callum arched a brow. "And *you're* avoiding the question."

"I'm not. I have nothing to avoid. You said I look terrible, but I'm fine." Slowly Theo took the other seat next to Callum, mostly because he knew if he didn't his friend would become even more suspicious.

Callum shook his head. "You're usually a better liar."

Theo caught his breath, and for a moment the two men simply stared at each other. He had known Callum since school, he trusted his friend. He had held him up during his own bad times and he had no doubt that the duke would do the same for him.

But what was happening between himself and Bernadette felt so very...fragile. Delicate. If he said the words, not only would Callum read into them, but they might shatter on the air. Disappear like smoke. And Theo didn't want to lose her. Not yet.

"Just leave it alone," he said at last.

Callum's expression softened. "Is it a woman?"

"What did I just say?" Theo snapped, startled by how much Callum could see. Was he so obvious?

Callum leaned back and opened his mouth, then hesitated and shut it again. He seemed to be reading Theo, gauging him...perhaps even judging him and Theo shivered beneath that weight.

"Is it Bernadette?" Callum finally pressed.

Theo didn't answer, but shoved to his feet and walked away, leaving the chair he'd departed to rock backward. It was only Callum's quick reflexes that allowed him to catch it before it clattered to the floor. As he righted it, Theo could feel himself being watched.

"I'm surprised that you're so shocked by the question," Callum said softly. "We *all* know there's something between you two."

Theo pivoted back. "What...what does that mean?"

Callum's brows lifted. "You are a new Theo every time she enters a room."

"That's rubbish," Theo said, and returned his attention to the garden below. He wished he felt the charge was as ridiculous as he claimed. But sometimes when he was with Etta he did feel...different. New.

He heard Callum's chair creak as his friend pushed to his feet behind him but still refused to turn back. He was already revealing too much, he didn't want to do even more. Didn't want to endanger himself or put Bernadette on the spot with her friends.

"Clearly you don't want to speak about this to me," Callum said gently.

"There's nothing to speak about." There was a long pause and Theo finally faced him. Callum was watching him so closely now and there was...God, was that a pitying expression? For what?

"Speaking from recent personal experience," Callum said. "Don't destroy something out of fear that could make you happy."

Theo wanted to say something pithy in return, meaningless words were right there on his tongue. Only he couldn't. He could only stare at Callum, who he knew had gone through hell and come out the other side with love and a future…and feel envious.

"Callum," he said, his voice rough in the quiet room.

But before he could say anything more, there was a light knock on the partially closed door and Kimball stepped partially into the room. "I beg your pardon, Your Graces, but the Duchess of Tunbridge has arrived. I've put her in the parlor, as you requested."

Theo nodded and Kimball stepped out. Now when he turned back to Callum whatever wild desire he'd had to confess his soul was buried again. It seemed Callum realized it, too, because he got to his feet with an expression of surrender.

Theo forced a smile and extended a hand to him. "I'll see you when you and Valaria return. How long are you gone?"

Callum still looked concerned, but he shook Theo's hand regardless. "Ten glorious days," he said, and looked vastly content. "Shall I say good morning to Bernadette, as well?"

He could see the questions in his friend's gaze but ignored it. "Certainly, if you'd like."

Callum inclined his head and they moved out of the study and to the parlor together. Bernadette was standing at the fireplace as they entered and she turned back, a bright smile on her gorgeous face. When she saw Callum, that smile dissipated and she caught her breath.

All of which Callum ignored, though he must have seen it, too. He crossed to her and took her hand. "Bernadette, I didn't realize you and the duke had an appointment. I'll leave you to it, but I hope I'll see you this afternoon for tea with Flora and Valaria."

She nodded. "Y-yes. To see you two off on your adventure tomorrow."

"Excellent." Callum squeezed her hand and headed back through the room with a meaningful look for Theo. "Good day, you two."

As he left, Theo reached behind himself and quietly closed the door. Etta tracked the movement, but there was little pleasure in her gaze, only fear as she stepped forward and said in a harsh whisper, "Does he know? Did you tell him about what we did?"

~

B ernadette watched Theo's expression close off at her question and his body language become more guarded. He arched a brow. "Do you fear that?"

"Of course I do," she said with a shake of her head. "A woman's reputation is so fragile. Even we widows must be careful."

He nodded slowly. "Of course. Although he would never do anything to hurt you, Callum knows nothing. He did say that he and the others suspect there might be something between us, but I gave him no details."

Even though that was exactly what she wanted in this moment, secrecy, there was a flash of disappointment that worked through her. After all, if Theo had told his dearest friend about their connection, that would mean it meant something to him.

Which it didn't. It didn't mean anything to either of them. She had to remember that if nothing else.

"They all...they all see things where they don't exist because they're in the throes of new love," she said, wishing she sounded steadier.

"Yes," he agreed, far too readily. Then he moved toward her and her heart started to throb. "This," he said, taking her hand and drawing her closer, "is between us."

He kissed her gently and she lost her breath. She wound her arms around his neck, feeling the same fire stoke in her today that had stoked in her last night when he had her in his arms. Everything else fell away, including her tangled feelings about a connection beyond the physical. She leaned into him, opening to him, loving when his kiss became more driven and reckless.

At last he pulled away, pressing his forehead against hers as they both panted with desire.

"And what is this?" she asked when she could find any words at all.

He drew back, searching her face. Then he took her hand and led her to the settee. "That is what we should decide. That's why you're here." She settled into a place and he moved away from her to the sideboard. "Would you like tea?"

"Something stronger, I think, despite the early hour," she gasped out.

He laughed. "You and I are of a mind. I tried to convince Callum to have a brandy with me earlier and he acted like I had lost my senses."

She smiled, feeling the wobbliness of it. "I could soften mine, at the very least. I'll take the brandy he refused."

"Excellent." He poured two snifters of what she guessed was his best and returned to the settee to take a place beside her. He didn't touch her, not when he handed over her drink, not when he sat down, but he never stopped watching her, even as he feigned being casual and took a sip of the alcohol.

"How do you usually hold these negotiations?" she asked.

He smiled and that, at least, was real. "I suppose I've never done so as formally," he admitted.

"But you think in this case that being formal is needed."

"Yes." He hesitated a beat and then said, "Etta, I know what I want."

She blinked. "You—you do?"

"Yes. I want to do what we did last night. I want to do it often. I want to taste you and touch you and please you over and over again. I want you sweaty and shaky in my bed, I want you moaning for more. I want to teach you new ways to drive me wild, to drive your-self wild."

Her lips parted almost against her will at the images that frank admission put in her mind. Of this man over her, under her, inside of her. "I see," she squeaked.

"But I also know exactly what that means and what it will look like and feel like when it happens. From our conversation last night, I think you don't have that same experience. So the real question, when we talk about the future of any affair we might indulge in, is what do *you* want?"

She swallowed. She'd spent a lifetime not being asked what she wanted. Her needs were rarely considered by the men in her life. So the idea of the freedom to decide on a path for herself was almost overwhelming.

"What are my choices?" she asked.

He finished his drink and set it aside, which left him free to rest his hand along the back of the settee. His fingers traced her shoulder lightly and she let her eyes flutter shut briefly because it felt so good.

"When you said that you wanted to take a lover the night of the wedding, it seemed like it was about one night of passion. A taste of what your friends had found. We had that last night, it was glorious. If that is all you want, that's fine. One night of pleasure, we return to being friends. No harm done, a happy memory for us both."

"But you said you wanted more," she whispered.

He shrugged. "We're not talking about me. Is that enough for *you?*"

She thought about the question, thought about last night, thought about how she'd awoken alone in her bed, still achy and needy for him. How she hadn't been able to stop thinking of him all morning.

After a long, shaky breath, she whispered, "Do you know how hard it is to sit here next to you?"

His brow wrinkled. "Is it?"

She nodded. She'd never been brave like this before, but the idea that she could lose what they'd started made her so. It made her want to be honest. So she was.

"When you're touching my shoulder like that, all I want to do is lean into you. When I can smell you, I want to taste you. If we stop at one night, I fear everything will be changed between us forever, no matter how I try not to make it so. Because I'll still want you, Theo." She dropped her gaze. "And I know that makes me a terrible wanton."

"No it doesn't," he said with a snort. "I asked you what you wanted. You're telling me. There isn't a wrong answer."

She wasn't certain he was right. Many people, after all, would insist that this entire endeavor was wrong. But Theo had never been like other people. That was always why she'd liked him so much. She liked him still.

"If you want more," she said. "I do too."

"Good." His fingers slid farther down her shoulder, playing along the hem of her short sleeve. "Do you know how long you want this to go on?"

"Valaria and Callum will be gone for ten days," she said. "And Roarke and Flora are always half busy with each other."

"Yes. Married for months and they still barely come up for air," Theo chuckled. "Though I don't blame them. That sounds perfect to me."

She couldn't fight the little smile that inspired. "If we are too wrapped up in each other, they'll see. You say they already do. Why don't we take advantage of a time when two of our group are gone and the other two might be busy most nights?"

"Ten days," he repeated.

She nodded. "When we reach the end, we can always reevaluate, see if we want to risk more."

"Very well," he said softly, his tone unreadable. "Ten days it is. And what do you want it to look like?"

She wrinkled her brow because she didn't fully understand the question. "Look like?"

"Last night I stayed in your home until dawn and sneaked out," he said. "Do you want our assignations to be brief? Do you want to spend nights together? Do you want to go out on the town before we retire? Do you want to make only one place where we meet? Do you want to return to the Donville Masquerade for our meetings?"

"Oh, I see," she said. "Goodness, that's a lot of detail."

"Specificity will help avoid misunderstanding and hurt feelings," he said. "Because one thing I do not want to lose is your friendship, Etta. You may not believe this, but it does mean a great deal to me."

That confession warmed her almost as much as his touch. Perhaps too much, considering how brief they were arranging for this to last. She would have to be careful.

"I don't want to lose yours either," she agreed. That, at least, she knew. "Could we mostly meet here?" she asked. "Kent's Row is not a large neighborhood and many of the dowagers who live there have little else to do but look out the window and notice everyone else's business. I fear our secret will come out if we meet there too much. And you…"

"I have a reputation and you believe my servants to be more discreet," he filled in effortlessly.

She nodded. "Yes. As for spending the night…" She pictured drifting off in this man's arms, of waking in them unlike she had that morning. It sounded like heaven. Dangerously so, even. "Er, why don't we assume we will sleep separately? Pleasure for the bed, sleep at home."

There was a moment when she thought he looked disappointed at that, but then it was gone and she must have imagined it, because he had claimed he wanted to explore more passion with her, but he couldn't crave the intimacy that sleeping together would create.

"As you wish, Your Grace," he said softly.

"I suppose it will be easy for you to keep things light…meaningless," she said.

He arched a brow and slid a little closer. "Not meaningless."

He leaned in, his breath warming her lips, and then they brushed hers. She gripped his lapels, sinking into him as he kissed her. Kissed her. Covered her and kissed her until her blood heated and sang, until her hands shook, until her body pulsed in time to her heartbeat.

But if she expected him to go further, she was disappointed. After the kiss went on for a while, he sat up and smiled at her. "I would love to take this so much further, but it seems you are joining your friends for tea."

"In a few hours," she said, realizing she was begging after the words had slipped from her lips.

"Ah, that's not nearly enough time for what I want to do," he whispered. "So why don't you run home, try to enjoy your day, and when you're finished...come back. Have supper with me here."

She shifted. "I suppose if I were late to tea or disheveled, they would only suspect something more, especially if Callum mentions that he saw me here with you. Yes, I'll come to you after."

"Good," he said, and then he caught her waist and dragged her closer once more. "I can't wait to take the next step."

His mouth found hers again, this time harder and it was like everything in her world expanded into stardust. Even when he let her go, she still tingled, still needed.

And she knew that when she came back, he would change her all over again. As terrifying as that fact was, she had no interest in escaping it, or him, until she had to.

CHAPTER 9

Because she intended to go straight back to Theo's home after
her tea with her friends, Bernadette was not wearing drawers.
It wasn't that she hadn't ever forgone undergarments—sometimes
the cut of a gown required it. But she'd never been as aware of the
fabric brushing her skin or the exposure beneath her dress as she
was now. She was keenly aware that as she sat so innocently with
her friends, as she had a hundred other times, she now had a
naughty secret.

So many naughty secrets.

"Look at this bevy of beauties," Callum said as he entered the
room with a broad smile.

Bernadette ducked her head and heat filled her cheeks at his
appearance and the way his gaze briefly flitted over her. Was he
simply acknowledging her or thinking about how he'd found her at
Theo's? If the second, how did he judge that? And would he say
what she hadn't come up with the fortitude to confess to her
friends, herself?

But he didn't. He chatted briefly with their threesome about the
roads and the weather. It was innocuous and Bernadette tried to

concentrate, but she just kept thinking about Theo and her promise to return when this tea was over.

"I'll leave you ladies to your time," Callum said at last, and leaned down to kiss Valaria briefly. "I'm sure my wife will miss you all during our little escape, as will I."

"Have a wonderful time, Callum," Flora said with a wide smile on her face. When Bernadette didn't say anything, still half-lost in her own thoughts, Flora lightly elbowed her.

It jolted her from her distraction. "Oh yes, I can't wait to hear all about your trip. Safest travels."

He smiled at them all and slipped from the room. When he was gone, Valaria let out a dreamy sigh. "Ten days alone with that man. Bliss," she said.

"You've earned it, too, the way you two had to sneak around for so long while your official mourning period ended," Flora said. "I will tell you from recent experience that there is no love like blissfully and newly married love."

Bernadette smiled at their twin giddy expressions, but she felt the sting of them, as well. She might be opening a door to pleasure with Theo, but it wouldn't end anywhere. It was limited fun and sensation.

"I'm very happy for you both," Bernadette said, and meant it.

"You realize that now that both of us are settled, we will turn all our attention to finding you the same happiness," Flora teased her, grabbing her hand and squeezing gently.

"Oh, I don't think so," Bernadette said with a little shake of her head.

"Please don't say that," Flora pressed and now her tone was serious. "I want so much to see you get the happiness you so richly deserve."

"But I *am* happy," Bernadette said. "I have a lovely home, wonderful friends, and despite his failings, Tunbridge settled me well, so I have no fear financially. I don't *need* to go searching for someone who does not exist. No, I don't think I shall ever again light up for a man the way you two do for your very lucky husbands. And I'm content with that."

She said the words, but she didn't feel content. Flora's concern was clear as her smile fell. But Valaria had watched the entire exchange with a more focused expression that Bernadette had tried to avoid. "You say you won't light up for a man, but I noticed today that you do have a little glow to you."

At last Bernadette jerked her face toward Valaria. One fine brow on her beautiful face arched in challenge. Bernadette had to be careful now. Theo had said that their group of friends suspected there was something between them, even if they hadn't guessed exactly what. And since she wasn't ready to reveal herself, these waters were dangerous to tread.

"I don't know what you mean," Bernadette responded. "If I have a glow, perhaps it is from the bit of sun that dared to peek out from the gloomy winter sky a few days ago. I took a little walk in the park."

"Sun glow," Valaria said, exchanging a quick glance with Flora.

Bernadette shrugged. "That must be it."

The teasing in Valaria's expression faded and she leaned in a little closer. "Are you certain you are well, dearest? This transition where both Flora and I have left the Row cannot be easy. Should I not go on this wedding trip with Callum? Should I stay, do you need me?"

Bernadette stared at Valaria and then Flora and her heart swelled with love for both of them. She knew how much this trip with Callum meant to Valaria and yet she would give it up for Bernadette's well-being. And she could see Flora would also do anything to secure Bernadette's happiness. That meant the world.

"You two are the kindest and best friends I could ever have, but I am fine," she assured them. "And what would make me happiest of all is to see you go off to the countryside for ten days with your husband. And for Flora to keep her happy smile thanks to Roarke. So *go*, you silly thing! Eat wonderful food and stroll around whatever beautiful place he takes you and spend far too many hours doing...what married people do." She blushed. It seemed she was becoming forward in all things. "Do not think one moment about me, I will be fine."

More than fine considering she was about to spend those same ten days in a bed with a very talented lover, herself. As Valaria and Flora giggled about that last suggestion, she joined in, understanding it a little more now that she had felt it. Now that she could picture what would happen next and how good it would be. In fact, she couldn't stop herself from picturing it and found her body reacting even when she didn't wish it to.

"Bernadette?"

She jolted as she realized Valaria was saying her name. "Yes, what was that?"

"I said that I knew we had spoken about tea, but perhaps you two would like to join us for supper?"

Bernadette shifted. "I actually have supper plans, I'm afraid." Both women looked at her in confusion and she forced a light laugh. "You aren't my only friends, you know!"

Flora gave a playful gasp and lifted a hand to her heart as if wounded. "Say it isn't so!"

"I'm afraid I have a very robust social life which I have been keeping from you both," Bernadette said even though it was skating dangerously close to the truth. The others didn't seem to notice, they just laughed at her teasing. "But I know you and I will see each other soon enough, Flora. And we'll do a gathering of all of us when Callum and Valaria return."

"We will," Valaria agreed with a wide smile. "Now I must ask you, Flora, where did you find the fabric for that gown? It is exquisite!"

Bernadette settled back as the talk turned to topics that were less fraught than love or passion or the future. And yet her mind still turned to Theo and what would happen in a few hours when she came to his home and their affair truly began.

Bernadette had mentioned, more than once, to Theo that he'd had a great many lovers. But as he sat at his desk, drumming his fingers along the great cherry wood top, he was trying to recall them all. It was an exercise not meant to be braggadocios, but more to settle his uncommonly unsettled nerves. He needed to remember that he knew how to do this, how to be in a physical relationship with a wildly beautiful woman and not let his heart get involved.

He needed the reminder because he was far too uneasy as he awaited Etta's return for their night together. He kept checking the clock, straightening his clothing, running a hand through his hair… Christ, he'd had to leave his bedchamber entirely because he kept moving candles around to find a perfect placement.

This was not him. This was not what he did or how he ever felt. He was put to mind of what Callum had said earlier in the day. That when he was with Bernadette, he was a new Theo. But he didn't want to *be* a new Theo. Did he?

"Your Grace?" Kimball said from the door.

Theo straightened. "Yes?"

"She has arrived, sir. All has been arranged. Supper will be served in half an hour."

"Thank you. She's in the west parlor, then?"

Kimball inclined his head. "Yes. Is there anything else I can provide?"

"No, you've been helpful, as always, Kimball. I appreciate you and the staff more than I likely express."

For a moment his butler's expression softened. Theo had known this man his entire life. Kimball had served his father, after all, before him. He'd always been a kind and steady presence. "Your

Grace, it is a pleasure," he said softly. "As is the duchess. Always so kind."

Theo tensed, not because Kimball wasn't correct—Etta was nothing but kind. She was kindness personified, a light that glowed out from inside of her and made everyone around her feel...safer. Better. More whole. Welcomed.

No, he tensed because he realized that his butler thought Theo was...*courting* Etta, though perhaps not in the most traditional way. Kimball believed she would one day have a place in this home, providing his servants with guidance, his halls with laughter and sweetness.

"Thank you again," he croaked.

Kimball's brow wrinkled but he didn't say anything further, just inclined his head and left Theo to his own devices. But Theo didn't want to be left to those, nor to his tangled thoughts. He was confusing this issue, somehow, conflating head with heart, body with soul. And the best way to avoid that was to march into that parlor and let the games begin.

Certainly he would recall himself once he did that.

He smoothed his jacket and exited the study, taking long breaths as he made the short walk to the west parlor, which connected to the dining room next door through a pocket door. He found Etta there, standing in the middle of the room, looking just as nervous as he felt. Somehow that was comforting and he smiled at her as he entered.

She didn't say anything, but crossed to him silently and wrapped her arms around his neck. He was stunned by the forward action but didn't fight it. He pulled her closer and kissed her. It was like they'd been separated for weeks, not hours, as she lifted into him with a shuddering sigh and returned his kiss with fervor. He sank into the feel of her, the sweet taste of her, the comfort of her. There was nothing else in the world right now but this.

And it would have been so easy to forget everything else and just take her upstairs for a night together. But to do that would imply a lack of control. He needed to retain his senses for a variety of reasons in this situation. So he managed to extract himself from her, loving how her pupils were dilated, how her breath was short as she stared up at him.

"That was a proper 'good evening,'" he teased.

She laughed and the tension in the room dissipated immediately. Despite the passion that pulsed between them, she was his friend again, one he valued, and that made it easier.

"How was your afternoon?" she asked as he walked to the side-board and pointed to the liquor there. "Oh, no, thank you. I want to keep my wits a little, at least."

"Wits are overrated, my dear," he said, and elicited another laugh from her. God, he loved doing that. Loved making her break into a wide smile that brightened her entire being. "And my afternoon was very quiet after a certain distraction departed my company in a cloud of vanilla musky sweetness." She blushed and it felt like he'd caught the moon. "How was yours?"

"Lovely," she said with a sigh. "Valaria is deliriously happy and excited for her excursion with Callum. I will miss her while she's gone, but to see her so content after everything she went through..."

"It's wonderful, I agree," he said, serious in that statement. Their eyes met and they both smiled, a shared joy for their dearest friends. "And wonderful that their leaving gives us a little privacy."

She shifted, uncertainty crossing her face. "I admit I'm surprised this is how you'd use that privacy. I thought you'd just sweep me away."

God, but he wanted to do just that. But again, the feeling made him out of control. He cleared his throat. "We have all night for what will come next. Why shouldn't we share a lovely meal together and not put pressure on what will absolutely come to pass?"

"I suppose," she said carefully. "But you said something to me the other day and I want to repeat it to you." He tilted his head and she moved toward him a step. "If you change your mind, if you don't want this anymore...I want you to tell me. If there is to be consent, it must be from both parties."

He stared at her, seeing how much that statement stung her by the worry on her face, and yet she made it anyway. A way to protect him. A way to give him an out he most definitely didn't want. But since he didn't think anyone had ever considered giving him that out...it meant something.

"You have my enthusiastic consent, Etta," he said softly. "I will prove that to you later. But waiting sometimes makes the surrender all the sweeter."

She gave a little shiver at the word *surrender* and his cock responded accordingly. Oh, he would give her surrender, demand it in return. But later. Later, when everything didn't feel so sharp. When he could regulate the wild beating of his heart.

The door between the parlor and the dining room slid open and one of the footmen appeared there. "Supper is ready, Your Graces, whenever you are."

He held out a hand to motion her toward the dining room. "Are you ready, Your Grace?"

"I am. Very ready."

He chuckled as he followed her in and watched her be helped into a seat just to the right of his place at the head of the table. He didn't want her far away and had asked for just this arrangement. He settled in and for a few moments it was all hustle bustle of dishes being placed and wine poured. Finally, though, the last member of the serving staff stepped away and they were alone again.

She smiled at the dish before her. "White soup with almonds and rice? This is one of my favorites."

"I know," he said as he picked up his own spoon.

She tilted her head. "You know? How?"

"I do pay attention, you know," he said, and though he had planned this meal so that it included a great many of Etta's favorite foods, now he felt exposed. There was a vulnerability to knowing someone and he hadn't fully taken that fact in until she was staring in wonder at him, her eyes bright with how much this meant to her. He wanted to push that vulnerability away. To shut the door to it and put the spotlight back on her. He waited until she'd taken a spoonful of soup, smiling at its familiar, favorite flavor, and then he said, "May I ask you a question?"

She nodded. "Of course."

"I've noticed you always refer to your late husband by his title, Tunbridge," he said.

She took another spoonful of soup, he thought to create a pause for her to collect herself. After she had swallowed, she said, "Yes, I suppose I do."

"But you aren't usually so formal," he pressed. "At least with people you know well or care for. I wondered if there was a reason why."

He could see how tender a subject he had hit upon by the way the light left her eyes. He almost regretted asking, because he realized how personal this was. It wasn't a way to build a wall, not really. He wanted to know the answer, more desperately than he was ready to admit, even to himself.

"Our marriage was rather formal," she began. He noted how she slowed the conversation by taking another spoonful of soup. Soon the bowl would be empty, though, and then there would be no buffer until the next course was brought.

"Because it was arranged," he encouraged.

"Yes. I suppose that was the reason at first. He was older than I was, it was arranged, we didn't know each other very well. All of those things were reasons it was distant at first. And I spent a great deal of time trying to console myself that those were the reasons it remained so. But you know, Flora's husband was far older than mine when they married. It was also arranged. And she loved him. So it's made me come to realize that it wasn't only the circumstances that kept us apart." She bent her head, sadness flitting over her expression.

"I'm sorry. I shouldn't have pried," he said.

She shrugged. "No. With what we're doing, I think it makes sense you would want to know. You've gotten me to reveal more about my marriage than anyone else already, actually."

He shifted as she pushed her now empty bowl away a little and instead began to worry the napkin in her lap. Her pain cut him. He wanted to soothe it. "Are you talking about the fact that he didn't attend to you...physically?"

Her cheeks flamed. "Yes."

"Did he ever...hurt you?" he asked.

"No," she said instantly, and it relieved him beyond measure. "Thank goodness for that. I've appreciated it all the more after knowing what Valaria went through. Though it wasn't out of some great concern for me. He was simply too indifferent to please *or* harm me."

"Always?" he asked, trying to wrap his head around a man who wouldn't want this woman. Who wouldn't see all her wonderful qualities and be drawn to them. Or at least not wish to spend a great deal of time exploring her pleasure.

When she shifted, he reached a hand to cover hers. At the same moment, the door opened and servants entered to change the courses. She pulled her hand away, placing them both in her lap with another blush. The bowls were removed and soon replaced with plates of haricot lamb, which elicited a swift smile from her as she saw it.

But he was still too attuned to her pain to enjoy that small pleasure. Once they were alone again, he said, "Etta, if you don't want to talk about this, we don't have to do it."

She swallowed and met his gaze, holding there a moment, searching. "You and I have long been friends, so I know I can trust you."

That trust, given yet again and in such a different circumstance, hit him in the chest, just as it had when it had simply been about her body. "You can," he assured her.

"And since this subject has already impacted how I react when you…when you touch me, I think you might deserve to know all of it. I just hope it won't change how you think of me."

"Never," he said and meant it down to his soul.

She pushed her food around her plate, and he could see her mustering her will to talk about this subject. She took a bite, chewed carefully and said, "Then I'll tell you everything, Theo."

CHAPTER 10

I n the time since Bernadette had met Flora and Valaria, they'd
had many conversations about their late husbands. She had
certainly given a few vague descriptions of her past with Tunbridge.
But now, sitting at Theo's elbow, his attention fixed entirely on her,
she wanted to give more. Wanted him to understand, because she
had the strangest feeling that he *would*. That she would be seen,
perhaps for the first time in her life.

It was a bewitching idea.

"I had...hopes when I married him. Tunbridge. George." Her late
husband's given name seemed so foreign on her tongue. "I knew
there had been some arranged marriages where love developed
between the two parties. I told myself I would love him. And that I
would give him no reason not to love me."

Theo winced at that statement but was kind enough not to interrupt her.

The next part was hard and she struggled with the words she'd
never spoken to any other person on this earth. "He hated any over-
ture I made toward him." She whispered it so it wouldn't be so
powerful. "He made it clear he didn't want my affection. He hardly
wanted my body at all, he treated it like a duty he was forced to

fulfill. I thought perhaps he wasn't interested in that sort of thing, that he wasn't built with passion as a driving force. But now…"

"Now?" Theo said, and he reached over to cover her hand with his.

It was such a simple action, one not born of desire or passion. This was comfort and she blinked at unexpected tears at the warmth of him, both physical and emotional. She was a fool to lean into it, but she couldn't help it.

"I discovered the Donville Masquerade in some of his letters I found while cleaning out a space in the attic," she explained.

"Oh," Theo said with a frown. "What kind of letters?"

"One from the club, itself, instating a ban on him for bad behavior." She shook her head. "I cannot imagine how awful he must have been to break the simple rules Mr. Rivers puts in place for the protection of all involved. But he did. And I realized when I was standing in the club last night, watching all those people crash together like wild waves of a beautiful shore, that Tunbridge *did* want passion on some level. Just not with…not with me."

She said that out loud and it felt like the air had been sucked out of her chest. Not because she cared about the late duke—that ship had long since sailed. But because his lack of desire for her was so patently clear now that it reflected her own internal thoughts about herself. It multiplied the feeling that she was unwantable. That she was forgettable.

But when Theo looked at her, she felt none of those things. He wanted her and that felt like the gift of this affair, of his presence in her life. He continued to hold her gaze and there was something in his expression that was so raw that it couldn't be real. She didn't understand it.

"Etta," he whispered.

The door to the dining room opened and the servants entered to take their plates. Theo held up a hand to stop them without looking at them. "A moment," he said. "We won't be having dessert."

The servants backed away and the door was shut again, leaving them alone. He lifted his fingers to her cheek and traced the line of her jaw with his fingers. "Come upstairs with me," he said softly.

She couldn't have said no under any circumstances, not when his dark blue eyes were holding hers with such desire, such certainty. He wanted her. That went a long way in erasing the ugliness of the past.

"Yes," she whispered.

He pushed back from the table and helped her to her feet. He held her hand as he guided her from the room and up to his chamber. She held her breath as he opened the door. She had been in his home several times in the last few months, since their little friendship group had spent so much time together. But she'd never been here.

They stepped into an antechamber with a writing desk and chairs before a fireplace. He locked the door and then pulled her farther into the room. Into the bedroom, and she caught her breath. Candles had been placed all over, though not lit. He frowned.

"We're ahead of schedule in my ardor, so my servants haven't finished," he said. "Allow *me* to prepare the room for you, Your Grace."

She watched as he walked over and lit a wooden splint from one of the flames in the lamp, then moved around the room to light the candles. He tossed the splint into the fire and then went about lowering the lamps so they were soon bathed in only fire and candlelight, which made everything softer and more dreamy.

He stopped at the edge of the big bed and took her in. Then he asked, "How do you want to feel, Etta?"

He'd asked her this same question the night before, it stunned her just as much now. She'd never had anyone in her life care so much about her reactions and emotions. But this man was entirely focused on both.

Still, she saw a flicker of something beyond desire to his stare. She'd seen it in the dining room, as well. She frowned. "I can tell you how I don't want to feel: pitied."

"I don't pity you," he said, immediately and with strength.

She wanted to believe him but folded her arms nonetheless. "Are you sure? When I told you my pathetic story, I thought I saw a flash of that emotion."

He shook his head slowly and now he did move toward her. When he reached her, he gently uncrossed her arms. He lifted one of her hands to rest on his shoulder as he kissed her knuckles lightly.

"If I pity anyone, it's him for being such a bloody fool. He could have had this with you all those years." His voice caught, but he remedied it so swiftly that she had to have been imagining it.

He kissed her palm without breaking eye contact, her wrist. She was getting dizzy as he continued, washed away in his warmth. And it wasn't just physically. She felt herself yearning for more than just his touch. That was dangerous. It could only end in pain.

She wanted to stop it. To go back to the pleasure and not think about her heart. So in her mind she rolled through their conversation from the night before, searching for a feeling he'd listed off during his first offer. Something that would take away the connection she couldn't want.

"Dominated," she burst out at last, almost without thinking of the consequences. Both his brows lifted in surprise, and she raised her chin in challenge. "You say you want me, that he was a fool for not wanting me. So I want to *feel* that. I want to feel your drive for me. That you would do anything to have me."

His nostrils flared a little and there was such a dark desire that came into his gaze that her hands started to shake. "*That* will be easy, Etta."

Before she could answer, he slipped his hand through her hair, cupping the back of her head, and tilted her face up. He took her mouth—that was the only way she could have described the way he kissed her. He took and her knees went weak at the passion of that action. His tongue drove, his other hand moved to cup her backside, draw her up tighter against him. It was rough and powerful and she felt like she could slip into this desire and allow him to just...take care of her.

But that couldn't be right, could it? When he broke his mouth from his, sliding to kiss her neck, she shivered. "What—what do I do?"

He lifted his gaze a moment before he did the same with his head. "Enjoy," he said softly. "You just do what I say and soak in the pleasure. You always have the power to say no. I will honor that no matter what. But as long as you like what I do, as long as you trust me not to take advantage of your surrender, then all you have to do is moan for me."

Her breath caught. "That's all you want? For me to moan?"

"You have no idea what that pretty little moan does to me," he said, massaging her backside harder, letting her feel the stiffness of him trapped between them and all their clothes.

She gave him what he wanted, she had no choice...she moaned. His chuckle was low and husky as he returned his mouth to hers and kissed her with the same drive. She felt him backing her toward the bed, stumbled when her backside hit the high edge, barked out a surprised cry when he toppled her onto her back, gripped the back of her knees through her dress and tugged her to the edge.

He held her stare as he pushed her skirt up, but when he reached her thighs he stopped and those blue eyes went wide. "Your Grace, you naughty thing, did you forgo undergarments?"

The heat of her blush made her cheeks feel aflame, but she managed to nod. "Yes, Theo. You told me not to wear them at a place like the Donville Masquerade—I assumed that meant you didn't want me to wear them if we were going to...to do this either."

"Anticipating my every desire," he murmured. "I don't know whether to punish you for being so bold or reward you for being so accommodating."

He straightened one of her stocking-clad legs and rested it against his shoulder. It made her dress fall higher, her legs open, and now she felt fully exposed. He bumped his hips against her bare sex and she gasped again.

"Would...would I like the punishment?" she gasped out.

He arched a brow. "You think you would?"

"I saw a gentleman spanking a lady's bare arse at the hell, and she seemed to like it very much," she admitted, and was surprised that her blush didn't grow even hotter. Perhaps she was just becoming accustomed to talking about such sinful things with this man. He made it safe for her to do so.

For a moment, pure shock flowed over Theo's expression. "You're going to kill me."

"What?"

"I just...didn't expect your sweetness to also be so very wicked," he said, and leaned in to kiss the inside of her calf, just below her knee. Even through the stockings, the damp heat of his mouth was magic against her skin. "Yes, to be dominated could mean a great many things. Some play games of punishment and reward and spanking might be part of that. Some participants like to be lightly choked."

"They do?" she said with a gasp. "Why?"

He shrugged. "The edge of pleasure is often close to the bite of pain. I can show you if you'd like."

"Maybe...maybe next time," she said. "I have to think about it."

She waited for him to become annoyed that she was denying him when he was supposed to be in control, but he made no show of that emotion. He nodded. "Whenever you like. Or never, if you prefer."

"Do you like to be choked?" she asked.

His little smile was an answer even before he said, "I've been known to partake in a little bite before the pleasure. It's never about hurting. It's about that feeling of a loss of control."

She nodded. "What else?"

"It could simply be me taking you very hard, very fast. Rough." His voice was getting hypnotic now. "Or withdrawing your pleasure until I choose to allow it. Keeping you right on the edge until you're mad with it. Sometimes it's a combination of all those things. Do you still want to be managed? Dominated? To surrender entirely to my whims?"

"Yes," she said, immediately and with strength. "I want that."

"Very good." He stepped back and shrugged out of his jacket, tossing it away without even looking where it landed. Then he untied and unwound his cravat. He looked like he was going to tug off the dangling edges of it and toss it aside, too, but then he looked at her, sprawled at the edge of his bed, dress still up around her hips, and he chuckled.

"May I tie you up, Etta? So you can truly give over to me?"

Her lips parted. Perhaps she should have been afraid of that idea, of allowing him such great power. But instead she was aroused. She nodded.

He tugged her to a seated position and reached around her back to unbutton her gown. Together they slipped it from her arms and she lifted her hips as he removed it from her body. Her short chemise was next. He tugged it over her head and threw it where his jacket had landed. That left her in just her stockings, her slippers.

When she moved to unfasten the garter, he shook his head. "Just the slippers."

He tugged off one, then the other, and they clattered with the rest in a disorganized pile. He smiled at her, naked, and motioned to her on the bed. "Move to the pillows, please."

She scooted over so she was resting in a normal angle on the bed. He finally slipped the silky cravat from around his neck and set it on the foot of the bed, then unfastened and pulled off his shirt. She felt her breath shift at the sight of him half naked again. It was really unfair how beautiful he was.

He swept up the cravat again as he put his knee on the bed and crawled up the length of her body. He pressed his mouth along the lines of her skin as he went. His tongue skimmed her knee, his stubbled cheek brushed her inner thigh. He paused between her legs, pushing her wider and gave a few languid licks of her sex.

She lifted against him with a cry she couldn't hold back and he looked up at her, slowing his tongue, teasing for a few moments more. Then he was on the move again, his fingers gripping her hips as he kissed the line of her pelvic bone. He nuzzled her stomach, then up between her breasts. Once again he paused and licked and sucked her nipples for a moment until her moans filled the air around him.

He started to move upward again, kissing her neck, her cheek, her ear. But not her lips. Instead he pushed up on his knees, and with swift efficiency she had to believe was born of practice, he wrapped one end of the cravat around one wrist, then pulled the length around a space in the headboard of the big bed. Her hand lifted above her head while he tied her other wrist the same way. The binds weren't tight, weren't uncomfortable, but when she tugged, they didn't move. She was trapped and he looked down at her like she was the dessert they had skipped to come to this room.

"This is just too perfect," he all but purred. "You are gorgeous like this, you know. Naked and spread out for a feast."

She shifted. A feast sounded very nice. She pulled against the bonds again and he clicked his tongue. "Now, now. You are tied up so that you don't feel compelled to try to run things. Just...surrender."

As he said it, he got off the bed and took his boots off, then his trousers. She stared at his already-hard cock, though this time she felt no fear in what he would do with it. All she wanted was to feel good and this man made her feel very good, indeed.

"Surrender," he repeated, and she realized she was still pulling taut on the cravat.

Slowly she let out her breath and relaxed, resting on the pillows, watching his every move like a bunny would a wolf. Only she wanted to be caught. Devoured, as he'd just promised he would. As he'd started a moment ago.

"Moan for me," he whispered while he moved back onto the bed and placed both hands on her calves. His fingers stroked along her skin, nails abrading lightly and sending electric awareness through her every nerve ending. She did as he'd demanded without hesitation, she moaned and his pupils dilated.

"Yes," he grunted. "Again, Etta."

Now he slid his hands higher, massaging her thighs, letting his thumbs smooth at the place where her bare skin met the pretty tied garters. How could that feel so thrilling?

She let out another moan and his pupils dilated. "Now come for me," he ordered, and dropped his mouth between her legs.

She cried out at the sudden stimulation between her legs. Where a moment ago he had teased, now he seemed focused and serious in every lick. He stroked her clitoris over and over, just the perfect pressure, just the right spot. She found herself tugging on the cravat again, this time because she wanted to put her hands in his hair. To touch him.

But she couldn't. She was at his mercy. That fact made her moan again as the sensation increased. She lifted her hips against him, grinding and reaching for the pleasure she felt just out of reach. It was building with every focused suck and lick, with every stroke of his hands against her thighs to hold her steady. He looked up at her as he licked, his dark blue eyes holding hers, filled with desire and pleasure and promises of what he could do if she just let him.

So she did, and when she surrendered, fully gave in, stopped thinking and only felt, that was when the sensation hit its peak. This time it was even more powerful. Long, hard waves of pleasure ripped through her, making her back arch, making her breathe hard, making her moan just as he'd told her to do.

He let her ride that pleasure for a few moments, increasing the pace of his tongue, keeping her hostage to release. But before the sensations faded, he rose to his knees and tore in half the cravat that bound her hands. She reached for him, but he didn't allow it, instead cupping her hips and flipping her over on her stomach in one sure movement.

He lifted her hips so she was on her hands and knees and then speared her with his cock. She gripped the pillows as the orgasm that still quaked through her intensified. She rippled around his hard cock as he took her just as he'd promised: hard and fast and rough.

And she loved it. Loved how he moaned and grunted in time to her own cries, loved the sound of their bodies slapping together. Loved how he held her so tightly that she knew she'd have finger bruises. He let go of control the same way she'd let go, and as she arched beneath him, he threw back his head and hissed out her name before he withdrew from her body and came against her back.

She expected him to flop over her, cover her with his heat and his power. Instead he turned her on her back once more and leaned down to lick her a few more times. She moaned with the unexpected attention, which sparked the remainder of her twitching release. At last, he licked one last long time and then moved to tug her against his chest.

She clung to him, their ragged breath matching in the quiet. When she could somehow speak again, she looked up at him. "Why did you do that?"

He shook his head. "Which part? Was there something you didn't like?"

His concern was plain on his face and she reached up to cup his cheek in reassurance. "No, I loved all of it. I meant…why did you go back to lick me after you were…finished?"

"Oh, that," he said with a faint smile. "I wanted to taste your pleasure, Etta."

She buried her head back against his shoulder so he wouldn't see her expression. She feared it revealed too much about what these moments meant to her. She couldn't share that with him.

He smoothed his hands over her arms and gently lifted her hand. "Did the cravat hurt your wrists?"

She looked and saw there was a little redness from where she'd pulled against the bindings, even though she didn't even remember doing so, she'd been so lost in this man.

"No," she said. "Not at all."

He kissed the discoloration. "Did you like it?"

She drew a shaky breath. "I did. Did you?"

"Mmm-hmmm," he murmured. "I like any way that I get to put my hands on you." He got up. "Now let me get a cloth and I'll help clean up the mess I made."

He kissed her gently and then got to his feet and padded naked to the basin across the room. She watched him prepare a cloth, wide-eyed at both the idea that he would take care of her like he was, and that she liked it so much.

And for a while, she pushed aside the fact that allowing this care was dangerous. Allowing her heart to beat faster for him, even more so. She would end it before it went too far, but for now she just wanted to enjoy it.

CHAPTER 11

B ernadette stared out the window at the gently falling snow and tried desperately to listen to Flora as she talked about a book they'd both been reading. She wanted to be attentive and open to her friend, but her mind was spinning.

She and Theo had been coming together for passionate assignations at his city estate for five days. Every night was wonderful, every touch was powerful.

And every time it was over, she gathered her things and left him, just as they had agreed. She was too afraid to ask to violate their rule and stay, even though some nights leaving that warm bed and his warmer arms was almost impossible. He never crossed that line either. But she tried to comfort herself that she was having the wild and wonderful affair of her fantasies and that was definitely enough.

At least that was what she told herself when she was alone and thinking of him and trying not to allow herself to go into thoughts of their friendship, of how well matched they seemed to be in other ways outside his bed.

"Bernadette?"

She jolted as she remembered herself. She'd come to Flora and

Roarke's home for tea with her friend after so many days of being "too busy". Of course, Flora had been equally entangled.

"My apologies," Bernadette said with a laugh. "I was clearly woolgathering."

"I would say you were," Flora replied. "I said your name three times before you jolted out of that dreamy state."

"You should be one to talk about dreamy, *Mrs. Desmond*," Bernadette said playfully. "If your husband so much as passes a door, you start batting your eyelashes and sighing like you're a heroine in some book."

Flora's cheeks pinkened and she ducked her head with a secret little smile. "Fine, I admit I am still distracted by Roarke and act a little like a romantic fool. So that's my excuse. What is *yours*, Bernadette?"

The question took Bernadette off guard, though perhaps it shouldn't have. She already knew her friends had suspicions about her friendship with Theo. They had suspicions about her odd behavior since even before Valaria and Cullen's wedding. And she'd kept the truth from them because speaking it out loud, especially the parts about Theo, felt...dangerous.

"If you think I'm dreamy, you're just seeing yourself through my eyes," Bernadette lied. "I think I'll get some more tea."

As she started to get up, Flora caught her hand, keeping her where she sat. She held Bernadette's stare for a moment. "Do you not trust me?"

Bernadette swallowed. "Of course I trust you. You are my best friend, both you and Valaria. And you and I have known each other even longer. I trust you."

"I can tell something is going on. Both Valaria and I can see it— your face is too open to easily lie. And I don't want to pry, I truly don't. If you tell me to sod off, I will and I won't bother you about whatever is happening. But perhaps I could help."

Bernadette was shocked by the tears that leapt to her eyes at those words. Why was she so emotional about this? She and Theo were very clear on what they had. What they didn't have.

Except that clarity of purpose wasn't exactly translating to a protection of her heart, which was her greater problem. She let out her breath in a wobbly sigh and stared at Flora. Perhaps there *would* be some good in talking about this. Flora might even have some advice on how to best remain detached emotionally.

And at least she wouldn't have to keep gripping this secret so tight to her chest where it sometimes felt like it hurt more than it helped. And the only other person she could talk to about it was Theo, which was an even worse idea.

"Fine," she said through lightly gritted teeth. "You aren't wrong. I have been…keeping something from you and Valaria."

Flora tightened her grip on Bernadette's hand. "If you want to talk about it, I'm here for you, dearest."

"I'm not sure how to begin," Bernadette said. "At Valaria's wedding, I suppose…or perhaps before that."

"Begin wherever you'd like." Flora folded her hands in her lap. "Take your time."

"For a long time, I accepted my life on Kent's Row," Bernadette started at last. "I was a widow, I had a life I enjoyed, and once you moved into the place and then Valaria, I was content that I had friendships enough to fill my heart and soul. But you two…ruined it."

"We ruined it?" Flora gasped. "How?"

"By falling in love," Bernadette said with a laugh. "Or I suppose more specifically by taking lovers. All of a sudden I saw you both awash in pleasure and excitement, and a door I'd long thought closed cracked open."

Flora's expression softened. "Oh. I understand. You wanted to be desired and have fun and play." She shook her head. "I know that feeling. When I started with Roarke, it did feel like someone turned a light back on in my life."

"Exactly, only there was no light yet for me. Just a desire to find it again. And so I…determined that I would find a lover."

Flora's eyes went wide. "What?"

"You judge me?"

"No, not at all, but allow me to be shocked." Flora grabbed her hand again. "You are the sweetest and sometimes the most innocent of the three of us. But I love that you got this idea in your head. It means you haven't entirely decided to surrender yourself to staid widowhood at all of twenty-eight. Did you…did you find someone for that purpose?"

"I…tried," she said, slower now because she'd reached the point where she'd have to decide if she wished to tell Flora about Theo, or just leave her lover as a faceless gentleman who made her toes curl.

Flora worried her lip. "Tried how?"

"I…went to a place called the Donville Masquerade. It's a hell specifically for, er, physical sin?"

Flora was staring at her, eyes impossibly wide. "Roarke told me about that place. You went there? What was it like?"

"Entirely hedonistic," Bernadette gushed. "Wild and wanton, I've never seen anything like it. But though I hate you and Valaria seeing me as innocent, in this I suppose I was. I felt over my head in that place, dizzy with too much stimulation. However, a gentleman did approach me, and I…we…"

"Bernadette!" Flora clapped her hands and then slapped one over her mouth when she realized how loud that exclamation had been. Together they giggled, and then she said more softly, "So you did take a lover. Despite your misgivings. He must have made you feel safe."

Bernadette lost her breath for a moment as her mind turned to Theo. Theo who always required consent for any new act, Theo who provided gentle care after any intense interaction, Theo who made her laugh even in the midst of passion. Just…Theo.

"He…he does," she whispered. "Very much so."

Flora's expression changed, all teasing leaving it. She tilted her head. "It's Theo, isn't it?"

Bernadette should have denied the charge. She should have told Flora she was being ridiculous. But all she could do instead was stare. "How—how did you know that?"

"The moment you two are in a room together, your connection is clear," Flora said. "It's electric."

"You simply see our long friendship," Bernadette said, but the words sounded weak to her own ears. "And I suppose that does help in making this new...this new connection a little easier."

"I've had many friends in my life," Flora whispered. "I've never become lovers with any of them."

Bernadette winced. She wanted Flora to help her strengthen her position that this affair would be nothing more than simply that. But she was doing the opposite. She was trying to make Bernadette lean to a side that was not safe and couldn't take her anywhere but pain.

She straightened up and lifted her chin. "Theo and I are lovers, nothing more. We've even defined the relationship as such and declared it won't last beyond when Callum and Valaria get back to Town."

"Why that date?"

"I suppose we were trying to avoid all of you nosy friends finding out what we were doing." She sighed. "So much for that."

Flora smiled a little. "My apologies for prying. Though....no, I'm not sorry. I'm glad to have found out this secret. And now I have other questions."

"Which are?"

Flora lifted both brows. "How is it?"

"It's..." Bernadette couldn't find the words to describe it. "It's marvelous, but that's not enough of a word to encompass it. He makes me feel so alive, Flora. Like I was sleeping all my life and now I'm wide awake. He can be tender, he can be bold, he can be wild, it's all about what I want or need in that moment."

Flora's expression softened. "That's wonderful, you deserve nothing less. And how do you feel?"

Bernadette shook her head. "I'm not sure I understand. Didn't I just say that?"

Flora caught Bernadette's hand and folded it so it rested on her own heart. "I'm asking how you *feel*."

And there was the most dangerous question of all. Bernadette moved her hand away from her suddenly pounding heart and shook her head. "Theo and I are friends, that hasn't changed. In fact, spending more time together has likely strengthened that friendship, which is very nice. But we've been clear with each other that to expect more would be foolish. I-I can't afford to be foolish."

"Because you have already been disappointed and you're afraid of having it happen again."

It was like Flora had stabbed her with that simple statement. Bernadette turned her head and stared blankly at the fireplace across the room. She drew a few long breaths. She wanted to deny that, to pretend it away, to build a wall but she found she couldn't. Flora was right.

"Yes," she whispered at last. "Exactly because of that."

They were both silent for a moment and then Flora said, "Bernadette."

She pivoted back to face her dearest friend and shook her head. "Please don't. I know what you want to say, what you and the rest of our dearest friends wish to have happen. But I can't. He won't. That is the end of it. I must be happy with this wonderful time we're having and accept that it is all there will be. All there can be. To hope for more or wish for more will only ruin the time I have right now."

Flora sighed. "I have so many things I want to say or encourage, but I respect that you know what is best for you."

"Thank you," Bernadette replied, filled with both relief and regret.

"Roarke and I are going to a play tonight and we're in Callum and Valaria's box. Why don't you and Theo join us?"

Bernadette pursed her lips. "After what we just discussed? What you're describing is courtship!"

"It is not," Flora argued. "You've come to plays and parties with Theo in attendance before."

Bernadette wanted to argue, but she blinked as she realized she couldn't. "I...oh, you're right. I suppose we have." Still, it felt different now. It would be different, even if she tried to deny that fact to her friend and to herself. "Fine. If you ask him and he wishes to do so, I'll be happy to attend. It would be nice to get out a little."

"Excellent! I'll have Roarke issue the invitation as soon as we're finished with tea. You can say good day to him, as well. I know he'd love to see you."

Bernadette nodded but sucked in a hard breath. "Flora...please... please don't tell him what you know."

"About you and Theo?"

"Yes. I-I don't want him to know. Or Callum. I will tell Valaria myself when she returns."

Flora looked a little confused by that request, but she inclined her head. "Of course. It's not my secret to tell and I won't if you don't want me to. Why don't I ring the bell and have him come in now? He can eat the last few biscuits and you can hear exactly what I say to him just so you feel comfortable, yes?"

Bernadette nodded and watched as her friend moved over to make the arrangements. But even though Flora was trying to make her as comfortable as possible, she still felt anxious. After all, the secret was now out. And in telling it, Bernadette feared she'd gotten a little closer to heartache.

One she would have to fight very hard to avoid.

CHAPTER 12

Theo hadn't planned to go to a play with Etta that night. No, his intentions had leaned more toward naked skin, a hot bath and their bodies intertwined for as long as she would allow it before she fled from his house and into the night.

But now, sitting in Callum and Valaria's box in the Theatre Royal at Covent Garden, he was actually happy to be out with their friends and her. It felt comfortable, right. *And* it gave him the chance to watch Etta under a far different circumstance than when she was arching beneath him in his bed.

While a great many attendees of plays talked their way through the entertainment and were there to be seen, not to partake in the arts, she was as different in this as she was in everything else. She leaned against the rail, watching the actors perform with rapt attention. Her eyes shone in the candlelight as she took in every word and movement.

She looked stunning. She wore a gorgeous blue gown with intricate stitching along the bodice and skirt that depicted flowers. Her hair was piled loosely on her head in a Grecian style. She was everything to look at and it was difficult for him not to reach over in the dimness of the box and take her hand.

He might have at that, if Roarke and Flora weren't right there, both watching them like they knew something was going on. He wouldn't feed their interest and create even more confusion to a situation that was already becoming more and more blurred by the moment.

The last line was shouted by the actor on stage and the stage lights dropped dramatically, signaling the end of the first act and the beginning of intermission. As servants scurried to light more candles and raise the illumination of the house, Etta smiled over at him.

"It's a very good play," she murmured.

He nodded, not adding he had no idea what it was about since he was too busy watching her. "Why don't we all go get some refreshments and be seen?" he suggested, not just to her but to their friends, as well.

Flora laughed. "We wouldn't want to miss that, would we, dearest?"

Roarke let out a little groan, which made their party laugh. He made no secret that he didn't love the social part of Society. Theo believed that Roarke would likely be perfectly happy to only be with his wife. He'd always thought that to be a silly notion, but now...

Well, the idea of being locked away with only Bernadette wasn't a terrible one. Of course, she wasn't his wife. She'd never be his wife. He'd known that when he was barely eighteen, hadn't he? He'd certainly gone over that night many times in the recent days. Thought about how he'd strenuously refused Etta's hand as a way to thwart his father and then briefly regretted it on the terrace later.

He always pushed the thought away and he did so now, instead offering her an arm to guide her from the box behind their hosts. When she took it, he thought her heard her slight intake of breath, but when he looked down at her, she smiled up at him like this was as meaningless to her as it was to him. Like it was just another night when they were out as friends.

One day that would be all they were again, and he didn't want to think about how that made him feel. Protocol insisted that Theo and Etta leave the box first, as they were of higher rank than their hosts, and he guided her out and down into the crowded hall where theatre attendees had flooded out. It was loud and bright after the dimness of the box.

"It looks like they're circulating with drinks," Theo said above the din. "Roarke, should we make the effort to get some for the ladies?"

Roarke turned toward Flora with a playful bow. "I shall go into battle for you, wife."

Flora laughed and immediately played along. "Be careful. I'll wait for you."

Theo glanced at Etta, but she kept her stare off to the distance, as if trying to make sure he didn't make the same jokes to her. He tilted his head toward the ladies, and he and Roarke left them, pushing their way through the crowd, nodding toward friends and dodging feathers on some of the ladies' massive headpieces.

"There," Theo said, pointing through the crowd. "There seems to be a larger table of refreshments if we cannot find a servant with a tray."

They moved there together and took turns pouring punch for themselves and their partners. Theo turned to go back, but Roarke caught his arm. "They're deep in conversation, mate," he said. "Best give them a moment."

Theo looked across the room and saw that his friend was correct. Flora and Etta were standing close together in what seemed to be intense discussion. Flora squeezed Etta's arm and Etta frowned, then continued to talk in what seemed an increasingly animated fashion.

He wrinkled his brow as a suspicion was born in him.

"I don't know what they have left to discuss after this afternoon," Roarke continued. "They already shared all their secrets."

"Secrets?" Theo said, his stomach flipping. "What makes you think they were trading secrets?"

Roarke shrugged. "I can always tell when they've been swapping tales I'm not supposed to know about. Flora has very specific ways for changing the subject and making up for keeping them from me. To be honest, I don't care. She can keep secrets, so long as they aren't important."

Theo could feel his face falling and he didn't have the energy to put the mask of joviality back on. He looked at Etta again across the room. She glanced at him and then ducked her head. But Flora... Flora kept looking at him, her gaze flitting over him. Then she pursed her lips.

Etta had told her about him. About *them*. He knew it as well as he knew his own name. And then she'd told Flora not to tell Roarke. Was that because she remained concerned about her reputation, as she'd mentioned earlier when she feared Callum knew the truth? Or was she embarrassed?

Worse...was it all just an unimportant secret? Flora clearly hadn't told Roarke, so perhaps it *was* unimportant. *He* was unimportant beyond a fun tumble Bernadette would recall with faint pleasure.

The idea of that stung far more deeply than it should have.

"Come, we'd best return," he said, hating that his voice was rougher. "They'll want their drinks before the second act."

Roarke looked at him with a strange expression but didn't argue, and simply followed him back to the ladies. By the time they reached Etta and Flora, the women had stopped discussing whatever it was that had seemed to trouble Etta. When he reached her and held out the glass of punch, she smiled up at him, her face all brightness and beauty again.

"Thank you, Theo," she said as she slid the glass from his hand, her fingers brushing his lightly.

The sting he'd felt across the room dissipated a little at that touch, at that look. Why had he felt it in the first place? They'd always been perfectly clear about what they were to each other, after all. There was no need to complicate things. If she wanted distance, especially in public, if she wanted no emotion...he could give that. He had to, if only to protect himself.

Not that he had feelings to protect himself from.

"Theo?"

He blinked as he realized Etta had been speaking to him. He slipped the mask back on, smiling at her with the same playfully flirtatious emptiness that he reserved for any lady who entered his sphere and returned to what he knew best: the game.

As the play ended and the audience clapped halfheartedly before they started the buzzing exit of the theatre, Bernadette glanced at Theo. She hadn't been able to stop herself from looking at him during the entire second act, no matter how much she had once been invested in the play.

She had felt something shift in him during the intermission. During the first part of the night, she'd felt the tension there between them in the darkness of the box. She'd felt him leaning toward her, sometimes physically but always in other more meaningful ways. He took every chance to brush her hand or whisper something close to her ear.

It was flirtatious, yes. Theo was incapable of not being flirtatious —it was his nature. But there was something...deeper to it. A connection that sang to something deep within her that she was trying to keep at bay.

But when he'd returned to her midway through the play, drink in hand and false smile on his face, something was different. She never would have claimed that she knew this man. Even though they'd been friends as children, even though they'd spent months in each other's company, renewing that bond and strengthening it. If asked, she would have asserted it was only a friendly acquaintance, at least until the first time he touched her.

But now she realized that she *could* see when Theo was

pretending with a person. She *knew* when he was acting a part and it felt like he was doing that now. With her.

His conversation was…oh, how could she describe it? Too light? Too empty? His laugh too loud?

It sounded ridiculous. It *felt* ridiculous. And yet as he motioned for her to take his side as they exited the box…but didn't take her arm this time…she knew she wasn't wrong. And she knew she didn't like it. She wanted to have that small, real part of this man who so often played a part in public. She wanted to feel the real Theo under it all, the person who wasn't carefully on display for the world. That piece had meant more to her than she knew.

She didn't think the shift would change anything. They would certainly go back to his home tonight and he'd seduce her, claim her with the same passion and drive for her pleasure that he'd exhibited for days and days now. But would she be brave enough to bring up the change she felt?

Would he admit to it if she did? Perhaps not. They had both claimed to desire something light and passionate and brief. Perhaps this new distance was his way of recreating lines that had become blurred between them. Perhaps she was making something out of nothing, in more ways than one.

They had made their way through the entrance hall and out onto the marble steps outside. Before her there was a crush of horses, carriages and people. Everyone was fighting for position to make their way home or to the next club or hell after the play. Gentlemen were comparing rank going back generations as they tried to claim their carriage should pull up next. Cyprians stood side by side with wives and debutantes, all of them looking bored and irritated.

Bernadette was being jostled from every side and it aggravated her when she was already on edge with these tangled, impossible thoughts about Theo.

She glanced back to find him a few strides away, still talking to Flora. Roarke had gone, perhaps to find Theo's driver in the crush of servants and rigs. Bernadette sighed and walked away a few steps, trying to find a bit of space to gather herself. She needed to gather herself or else she would be too vulnerable in the close carriage.

She pivoted and stepped around the laughing, half-drunk patrons until she was just on the edge where walking path met the street. She drew in a few breaths, but the air was so close and it stank of horse. She frowned and stepped even farther from the crush.

Not far enough, it seemed, because a big, rather drunk man staggered into her in that moment. His heavy weight was not something she could fight against, and she found herself pushed forward, off the little ledge of the walking path and into the muddy street.

It wouldn't have been so terrible for it to happen—the carriages were all coming slowly, after all, and people were scattered everywhere. But at the moment she stumble-stepped into the road, itself, a horse made a terrible, screeching sound from her left. She pivoted toward it and the world suddenly moved into horrible slow motion.

The animal had been spooked by all the commotion, it seemed, and it reared up on its back legs, dropping its rider into the street. It slammed down onto its front feet to the screams of the crowd, its eyes wild and its head flipping back and forth in agitation. With no one to control it, the animal began to run at full speed right toward Bernadette.

She was frozen in terror, frozen in the knowledge that she'd never move fast enough to avoid injury, perhaps even death.

And then she felt a hand grip her arm. She was yanked back none too gently just as the horse crossed the exact place where she'd been standing. She stumbled away, tumbling in unison with her savior onto the hard surface of the pathway. She pivoted and found it was Theo who had grabbed her. He hit the ground with a grunt and tugged her in closer to his chest as if to further protect her from injury.

People were screeching at the near fatal accident, men were running to catch the horse before he hurt himself or others, she saw

Flora rushing from the steps toward her, her expression twisted in horror.

But the only person who mattered in that moment was Theo. Theo, whose strong arms were wrapped tightly around her, his body trembling and his face lined with...fear. He looked terrified as he held her so closely that she could feel his racing heartbeat even through all the layers of their clothing. He looked what she couldn't feel until he whispered, "Bernadette."

And then she broke down.

CHAPTER 13

Theo couldn't breathe as he held Etta tight against him, her body shaking and silent tears streaming down her face. His mind spun, thoughts of watching her step farther and farther away. It had made him uncomfortable to watch it, though he hadn't understood why. He'd been starting toward her already, just at that horrible moment when the horse had come full speed toward her.

He had felt the wind across his face from the animal barreling by as he'd barely snatched her to safety, he'd known just how close they'd come to tragedy.

And he knew something else, too, as she gripped his lapels with both hands and let him hold her: he was in love with her.

That had become sharply, brightly, perfectly clear in that moment when he'd thought he wouldn't reach her. In that flash of a moment there had been so many regrets that had filled his mind and body, there was that fact. He loved Bernadette.

That discovery still rang true as he slowly sat up and brought her to a seated position too. The crowd was moving in, both concerned and enraptured by the drama, whispering about the save as if it were part of the night's entertainment, some kind of great romantic revelation.

They didn't know how right they were.

"Are you hurt?" he asked, hardly recognizing his own voice.

"N-no, I don't think so. Just bruised a little," she whispered, and then she shook her head. "Oh, Theo."

He might have said something then, words that weren't meant for public consumption were on his tongue, but Flora reached them. Roarke was running from further up the street where he'd been seeking Theo's carriage. Hands of strangers and acquaintances were pulling him to his feet, and away from her as some of the women carefully examined her torn, dirty gown and her scraped hands.

"A good show, Your Grace," one man was saying as he patted his back. "The lady would have been killed for certain."

"They ought to monitor these events better," another was groaning. "There is a way to release the vehicles and animals, isn't there? They ought to do it by rank."

Theo pushed away from them. He was still too shaken to be angry that one of them was upset about rank not the fact that Etta had nearly died. He couldn't even see their faces as he stared at them. They were blanks as wave after wave of emotion poured over him: terror, pain, relief, love. It was overpowering.

"Fetch Lightmorrow's vehicle, for pity's sake," someone called out at last. "So the duchess and their party might go home."

The crowd parted, and Theo watched in numbness as his rig pulled up through the fray. His servants must have seen the near miss, as well, for they looked shaken as they climbed down. His footman helped Etta into the rig first, then Flora followed and Roarke went last, with only a brief glance toward Theo.

He shook his head and tried to get himself back together. If he got into the carriage like this, it would be too obvious. He wasn't ready for the feelings ripping through him like wildfire to be obvious.

"Go to Mr. and Mrs. Desmond's home," he directed his driver. "And then we'll be on to my home unless I tell you otherwise."

"Yes, sir," the servant said. "Are you sure you're not injured, Your Grace? That was a hard fall."

Theo almost laughed. "Harder than you know. But I'm not hurt. At least I don't think so."

And as he got into the carriage, he knew he wasn't talking about physicality. Which was terrifying.

∾

The carriage was deathly quiet as it rocked its way back to Flora and Roarke's home. The ride seemed to be taking forever, or perhaps Bernadette just felt that because she was so keenly aware that everyone's focus was entirely on her.

Flora sat on the same side of the rig as she was, holding her hands gently. Every once in a while she smoothed her thumb near Bernadette's scraped knuckles and winced as if it hurt her just to see the injury. Her friend's face was tear-stained and she took a gulping breath of air like she was trying not to cry all over again.

Roarke sat across from his wife, his face lined with concern for both her and Bernadette. Every so often he shook his head and shuddered, like he was reliving whatever he'd seen from his vantage point.

But it was Theo who kept drawing Bernadette's attention. He sat across from her, his gaze never leaving her face. He'd said nothing since he entered the carriage, hardly anything more since he'd saved her life. His expression held no clues to his thoughts or feelings. To see him without even an ounce of levity or emotion made her stomach turn.

Just as thoughts of what had nearly happened did. How could something be so fast and so slow all at once? And why did her heart race all over again when she pictured that galloping horse getting larger and larger as it rose up to run her down? It was over. She shouldn't be afraid anymore. It would only make it harder for everyone else.

The carriage slowed as it turned onto Roarke and Flora's drive. That seemed to wake everyone up. Flora reached up to cup her cheek. "Dearest, why don't you come in? Have a drink. We can clean up those scrapes and I'll help you check your bruises. You could even spend the night here. I hardly want you to leave my sight after such a fright."

Tears stung Bernadette's eyes at the sweetness of that offer. She'd long considered both Flora and Valaria to be like sisters, but this took that feeling even further. "I adore you for caring," she began, squeezing Flora's hand gently. "But after tonight, I think I just want to go home. I want to rest."

She glanced at Theo as she said those words and knew she wasn't going home, at least not any time soon. Even when his expression didn't reflect his feelings, his eyes told her that.

"Theo will take me," she said, and felt a little heat touch her cheeks. Flora knew about the affair, of course, but she had to assume that Roarke would guess the same after everything that had happened tonight.

Perhaps it didn't even matter.

"Are you certain?" Flora asked softly with a quick glance of her own at Theo. He turned his face and looked out the window as they resolved the issue.

Bernadette nodded and tried to put on a brave expression. "I am. We'll talk tomorrow, I promise."

"Very well," Flora said with a sigh, and leaned in to kiss her cheek. "I'm so glad you weren't hurt," she whispered close to her ear.

Bernadette nodded, those tears returning even as she tried harder to keep them at bay. "Good night, Flora."

Flora slipped away, letting one of Theo's footmen help her down. Roarke hesitated a moment before he followed. "We are truly lucky, Bernadette. And grateful. Good night." He pressed a hand to Theo's knee before he, too, departed the cottage and shut the door behind himself.

They were alone again, though Theo didn't move or say

anything even as the carriage began to move. She drew a ragged breath. "Theo—"

He swallowed. "Come home with me."

She blinked. "Is that where we're going?"

"Yes." He nodded. "Unless you don't want to."

"I want to," she whispered.

There was a moment where his chin wobbled a fraction. "Will you stay with me?"

She caught her breath at that request, one that went against everything they had agreed to. "Theo," she said again.

But he was already moving, uncoiling from his stiff position on the bench across from her to kneel before her on the carriage floor. He leaned up and gently cupped her cheeks, searching her face like he was looking for something he'd lost. Then he leaned in closer. She felt his breath touch her lips and her eyes fluttered shut. She met him halfway for the kiss.

If his hands on her face were gentle, the kiss wasn't. It wasn't rough, but it was desperate. She felt that from herself as she tried to forget that she might have died tonight. She felt it from him, as she assumed he lived through those same moments. He delved deeply, like he was trying to prove to himself that she was really there. Really whole. And she let him, gave back as good as she got. Let him sweep her away so the sharpness of fear faded just a little.

"Please stay with me tonight," he repeated against her lips. This time his voice was shaky.

She nodded, felt her skin brush his they were so close. "Yes."

He softened then, leaning forward to rest his forehead on her shoulder as his arms came around her. She felt the air come out of him, almost like he was collapsing, and she clung to him to hold him up. Felt him hold her up in return. And they rode the rest of the way to his home like that, keeping each other upright.

As if they could support each other forever. She just had to remember that they couldn't.

~

T heo eased up onto the bench next to Etta as they made the final turn into his drive. He tucked her into his side, loving the feel of her head coming to rest on his shoulder. The carriage came to a stop, but he didn't pull away as he felt the wobble of the footman coming down from the back of the carriage. Through the window, he also saw his driver come bounding down. He raced to the top of the stairs where Kimball was exiting the house to welcome Theo home and the two men talked. He could see Kimball's expression grow worried.

At least he wouldn't have to explain what had happened to the house staff. He didn't think he could say the words out loud anyway. They were too raw and harsh.

"Can you come down on your own?" he asked against her hair.

She fisted her hand against his chest. "Yes. Thanks to you, I wasn't injured, Theo."

He lifted that same hand to his lips and brushed them against the scrapes on her knuckles. "You weren't *badly* injured." She didn't say anything and the footman opened the carriage door then. "I'll get out first and help you."

She nodded as he reluctantly released her and came down from the rig. He waved off the footman and extended his hand to her, steadying her with as much care as he could as she exited the rig. She took a deep breath of the night air. From the glow of the house, he saw that her hair had come half-down on one side, probably from when she'd hit the ground. The sleeve of her gown was torn almost completely off and the skirt was now spotted with mud and God knew what else from the pathway.

He pursed his lips and took her hand, guiding her up to where Kimball waited, his expression heavy with concern. As they entered the full light of the foyer, the butler's eyes grew wide. "Oh, Your Graces," he whispered. "Richards told me a bit of what happened. Are you both well?"

"We're fine, Kimball," Theo said, reaching out to squeeze the old man's arm gently. "Shaken, but seemingly uninjured, though I don't know how that is possible."

"Do you need anything?" Kimball asked. "I can have some food readied or drinks or tea or—"

"No, you dear man," Etta interrupted with a shaky smile. "Nothing."

Theo leaned in closer so she wouldn't have to hear his next direction. "Clean water, strong whisky and some extra cloths, please. You can put it all in the antechamber."

"Immediately, Your Grace," Kimball said with a quick nod before he hustled away.

Theo looked at her and she seemed so small in that moment. Like she'd shrunk with her fear. She was clearly still wobbly and tears filled her eyes often, though she always blinked them away rather than let them shed.

He gently took her hand. "Do you want to go into the parlor for a while or—"

"Your chamber," she said with a shake of her head. "I just want to go upstairs and not have to...to...pretend to be well."

He sucked in a breath. "Of course."

He led her upstairs and into his bedchamber. He closed the door and heard servants enter the antechamber behind him, preparing everything he had asked for. He would fetch it all in a moment, but for now he just stared at her. She paced past the bed and to the window, staring out at the garden behind his house.

"You must have been terrified," he said softly.

She didn't turn. "I was," she admitted after what felt like an interminable pause. "But I...I shouldn't trouble you with that."

He took a long step toward her. "Etta, it isn't troubling me if you share your fear or your upset. I want to hear it. I want you to be able to let it out."

She did face him then, slowly, her dark gaze flitting up and down his body. "You are so different from my husband, Theo. He would have blamed me for being so foolish as to stand close to the street. He would have said that I brought it on myself. That what happened or nearly happened was a consequence of my own bad choices."

When she said the last sentence, he realized she was not repeating the berating her bastard of a husband would have said, but punishing herself for what she'd done or not done that night. He closed the distance in two long steps and gently cupped her cheeks.

"It wasn't your fault," he said. "It could have happened to *anyone* on that street. It was a series of unfortunate actions that nearly..." He couldn't finish that sentence and turned his head.

"Nearly caused you harm," she said for him.

He blinked down at her. "You are worried about me?"

"Yes," she said. "Of course. You put yourself at risk to pull me to safety. What if you had—"

"Don't," he interrupted, and leaned down to kiss her briefly. "Don't." She let out her breath in a shuddering sigh and reached back to steady herself on the window ledge. "God, you look exhausted. Come, let me help you out of those torn clothes," he said.

She didn't protest as he drew her closer to the bed and turned her around so he could unfasten her gown. It wasn't the first time he'd done so, of course. She'd been coming here to his bed night after night in the past week, he'd taken off her gown many times, but this was different. He wasn't trying to seduce her—he was taking care of her. And he had admitted to himself that he loved her, and so as he gently unbuttoned her, it was like seeing her for the first time.

He pulled the gown down one arm and then the other, wincing as he noticed her scraped elbow and a rapidly forming bruise on her shoulder. He pulled her dress down around her hips and it swished at her feet. She turned to face him in her short chemise and pretty stockings, which were now torn just around where her knee was bruised, her slippers filthy with both dirt and a little blood from a cut on the top of her foot.

"Jesus," he breathed.

She shook her head. "It's not that bad."

He frowned. "You are cut and bruised all over your body," he said. "Please don't minimize that for my benefit, I have eyes."

At that, the tears she had been fighting not to shed began to slide down her cheeks. She made no move to wipe them, just stared at him as they fell. He took her hand and held it, wanting to wrap her up in his arms, but knowing that what she might need was just to let it out for a moment or two.

And she did, her breath becoming shorter as she whimpered, "The horse just came so fast. I wanted to move but I couldn't. It was like being in a dream."

"A nightmare," he said with a shudder.

She sobbed, "A horrible nightmare."

And with that she stepped forward into his arms. He smoothed her hair, letting her cry into his chest until her breath became steadier. Then he retrieved a monogrammed handkerchief from his pocket and gave it to her.

"Let me get the items from the antechamber. Why don't you sit by the fire?"

She did as she was told and he heard her blow her nose as he exited the room. Kimball had arranged everything Theo had asked for on a tray, and he carried it in and set in on the table next to the basin in his room. Etta had taken a place on the settee by his fire, half collapsed on the pillows while he was gone. He could feel her watching him as he filled the basin and then dipped a clean cloth into it, rung it out and turned back to her.

"May I tend to some of those scrapes?" he asked.

She nodded, watching him as he returned to her. For a moment he considered sitting beside her, but he would have a better angle on his knees, so he took to them, ignoring the soreness in his own muscles as he removed her slippers and set them aside, then glided his hands up to untie her garters. She took in a short breath as he did so and he supposed she must be thinking of the last time he'd done this.

With his teeth.

He glanced up at her and gave his cheekiest smile to ease her mind. "You were so kind to tear these to shreds. It gives me so many ideas."

She laughed a little and he was relieved at the sound. It meant she wasn't entirely broken by what had happened. "I would have much preferred *you* tear them."

"Yes," he agreed, and tossed each stocking away. He dabbed at the scrapes on her feet. She gripped the edge of the settee and hissed out her breath. Once again, he was struck by the dichotomy of forcing that sound from her lips with pleasure versus this.

He continued to wash each scrape on her feet and legs, then got up to rinse the rag and switch to a new one. When he returned, he sat next to her and went to work on her hands and arms. When she winced or grumbled with the pain, he felt like he was being stabbed, himself.

"I'm sorry," he said at last, without looking at her face.

"Why?" she asked. When he didn't answer, she slid a finger beneath his chin and forced him to look at her. Her expression was so gentle, so warm, so very...her that he almost couldn't breathe. "You saved me."

"But I should have protected you," he said, and his mind took him back, once again, to that night on the terrace so many years ago. When he could have saved her, truly saved her, from all the pains she had suffered in the intervening years. When he could have married her.

"That wasn't your responsibility," she said.

The images faded and he winced. He knew he loved her. Every time he thought of it, the emotion grew stronger and more insistent. More than that, he knew he wanted to do something about it. It was such an odd desire, after a life where he tried to avoid such attachment so strenuously.

But right now, Etta was still putting up walls between them. Perhaps they were because she only saw him as a friend...a friend who occasionally made her twist and moan with pleasure…but a friend. Or perhaps it was because she had never been given what she deserved when it came to her heart. Perhaps it was because she feared leaning into him if she thought she might fall.

And if that was the case, there was hope. If that was the case, he could prove her wrong and perhaps, just perhaps, work this out.

He got up and set the now dirty and bloody clothes in a pile to be taken away. He smiled at the whisky Kimball had placed on the tray. Theo's best. He poured a small amount into a glass and brought it back to her.

"Drink this, it will make the pain a little less sharp. And then let's get you to bed."

She gave a small laugh as she took the glass and dutifully sipped from it. She pulled a face at the strength and then choked out, "I fear I won't be the most strenuous lover, Theo."

He wrinkled his brow. "I just want to hold you, Etta."

She stared at him, the empty glass going slack in her hand. She looked confused by that statement, uncertain. But then she nodded. "I'd like that."

He pulled the covers back on the bed and as she climbed in, he stripped out of his jacket and sat down to remove his scuffed boots. His trousers and shirt were clean enough, and once he was barefoot, he got up and turned toward the bed.

Once again, he was struck by how small she looked in his bed. Shrunken by fear and worry. He took his place beside her under the cool sheets and drew her to his side, wrapping his arms around her, holding her. Her hand fisted and released against his chest, her body trembled, but she didn't weep again. And slowly, with the rhythmic tick of the clock, he felt her relax, felt her drift into sleep.

But he stayed awake. All night. Watching her breathe. And thanking whatever deity had intervened and kept her alive.

CHAPTER 14

Bernadette woke slowly, drifting in and out of dreams until at last she found herself staring at the ceiling above her. Her body ached, stiff, and it reminded her of everything that had happened after the play the night before.

Including that she'd spent the night in Theo's bed. His remarkably comfortable bed. The only thing wrong with it was that he wasn't in it with her.

She sat up and winced with the dull pain that echoed through her body. Slowly she moved all her joints and limbs, checking for injuries she might have been too shocked to notice the previous night. She was relieved when she didn't find any. She'd been lucky to escape with only the scrapes and bruises that Theo had so carefully tended to the previous night.

She flopped back on the pillows with a shake of her head. They'd made their rules of this affair, trying to keep things as detangled and simple as possible. She'd *wanted* those rules between them so that nothing became confused, so that she didn't start wanting things she couldn't have.

And yet he'd asked her to stay last night, hadn't made love to her, but simply held her. Was that out of fear? Out of pity? Out of guilt?

Her stomach turned at the idea that she had inspired any of those feelings. That he might only be with her because he now couldn't find an escape route after the accident he'd bravely prevented.

She was about to get up when the door from the antechamber opened and he appeared. When he saw she was awake, he came to a complete stop and just stared at her. Her breath caught. He'd changed out of his clothing from the night before at some point while she slept. He wore a dressing gown but clearly had little under it, because it hit him at the knees and his legs were bare, as were his feet.

She had seen him naked before, of course. She'd very much enjoyed exploring his body while naked. But this felt *different*. It felt...more vulnerable in some way? Because he was just going about his day, and she had no claim on that part of him.

He drew a little breath, then adjusted the tray he carried, laden with food. He carefully set it down on a table across the room before he moved toward her, his expression almost as unreadable as it had been the night before. Carefully unreadable, and again she shuddered at the idea that things had changed so much between them in one night.

"Good morning." His voice was soft, almost hesitant.

She reached out a hand and he took it as he reached her. She expected him to tumble down beside her, but he didn't, he just stood over her, watching her. There was a pulse of tension between them, and for once it wasn't sexual. It felt...deeper, and she shoved that thought away violently.

This was exactly why they'd made their rules, exactly why they had each declared that this thing between them was only physical. If she misread it now, saw it for something else, she was bound to be hurt. She was as afraid of that as she was of the galloping horse that had nearly taken her life the night before.

What she knew she could trust with this man was passion. It was the only way she could connect with him that didn't feel...fraught. Dangerous to her heart. And even that was, if she were honest. But in this moment, it was all she could demand or expect. The only way to balance the scales that felt off.

She tugged his hand and he stumbled forward onto the bed, into her arms. She slid her hands into his hair and drew him closer to her, taking his mouth just as he'd taken hers so many times in the last few days. To her relief, there was no hesitation to his response. He melted against her with a possessive growl, shifting his weight so he could hold her.

For a while, that was all they did. Kiss and kiss and kiss until she couldn't remember or feel anything but him and this. But eventually, he pulled back a little. Their faces were still close as he murmured, "Are you certain you want this, Etta?"

"This is what we are, isn't it?" she whispered.

There was a moment of hesitation in him again, and her heart raced with anxiety. Why did his expression change? Why did his breath hitch? Why did his mouth tighten?

He shifted a little, removing a bit of his weight from her. "After last night, I just want to be sure you feel up for it."

"Why wouldn't I be up for it?" she asked. "I wasn't badly injured. You must have as many bruises as I do."

He didn't answer that charge, but pressed his lips to her jawline almost absently. "It's not about the injuries. I don't want you to push too hard after that kind of fear."

She swallowed hard, that fear he was referring to flickering a little in her mind. Memories racing, mixed with her tangled emotions about this man. Then he kissed her neck gently and some of it faded.

"I-I was afraid, of course," she whispered, because saying it too loudly felt like it would conjure something she didn't want to face. "Terrified," she corrected, then she tilted her head and he lifted his own, and suddenly their eyes were locked. "But you kept me safe."

The moment the words left her lips, she longed to take them back, because something shifted in his expression. A wash of emotion flooded over him, though she couldn't tell if it was positive or negative because he erased it so swiftly. She expected him to pull away, to even remind her of the boundaries of their affair.

But instead he lowered his mouth back to hers, and just before he kissed her again he whispered, "I want to make you feel safe, Bernadette. Always."

Always was such a loaded word, but she forgot about that, forgot about everything but him when his hands began to move against her body. While he kissed her, he slid his fingers down her side, bunching her thin chemise against her body. When his palm cupped her bare hip beneath the blankets, she couldn't help but gasp against his mouth.

He'd touched her skin so many times—how could every time be so new? So powerful? She had no answers and no way to fight against his arsenal when he deepened his kiss and slid his hand around and behind her backside to lift her a little against him.

She moaned, flexing her hips higher, trying to find him through all the layers of the blankets that separated them. He smiled against her mouth and pulled away, getting back to his feet. As she stared at him through a hooded gaze, she saw that he wanted her. His dressing gown was tented with the proof. When he removed it, he was hard, curled against his body.

She pushed the covers away and pulled her chemise over her head so that she was naked too. His gaze moved over her and she felt on steady ground again, at least for a moment. When he looked at her like he wanted her, at least she understood that and what it meant for them.

But then she saw a huge bruise on his arm and she caught her breath. "Oh Theo!"

He shook his head. "If you aren't injured, neither am I. And right now I can't feel pain, Etta. There's only you."

He returned to the bed, shoving the blankets away the rest of the way as he covered her once more. She wrapped her arms around his broad shoulders, dragging her nails lightly against the skin and loving how his kiss grew wilder when she did so. But if she expected a quick, passionate joining, that didn't seem to be what he had in mind.

He moved his lips back to her throat, sucking and nibbling and licking like they had all day to do this. A bewitching thought, indeed. He drew lower, kissing her collarbone, grazing the bruise on her shoulder with his lips, sliding lower until he reached her breasts where he paused.

He glanced up at her, watching as he slowly circled one nipple with just the tip of his tongue. Immediately, heated sensation raced through her, but of course he'd known it would. They'd established in all their nights together that even the barest touch there would send her arching and moaning beneath him. Sometimes it felt like a game or erotic torture when he languidly spent his time here.

This morning was no different. He smiled against her, increasing the pressure of his tongue, lapping her gently and repeatedly. She dug her hands into his hair, grinding against him in an attempt to get some relief from the magic he was creating. He made a low sound in his chest, pleasure that matched her own even though she was hardly touching him.

He shifted to her opposite nipple, sucking gently, harder, until she started to shake beneath him.

"Oh, that is unfair," she murmured, laughing a little.

He smiled again and lifted his head. "How is unfair?"

"Because you know what you do to me. You torment me so mercilessly."

"God, you're pretty when you pout," he teased, then he sucked her nipple once more and started a trail down her ribcage. She opened her legs wider, twisting a little when he kissed along her hip. He hesitated and she opened her eyes to see why. He was looking at the bruise there, the heat fading from his stare.

"Theo," she whispered, drawing his attention away from the mark. "I can't feel pain. There's only you."

He started a little at her repeat of his earlier words, but then he nodded slowly and dropped his mouth back to her thigh, curving along the top edge before he nuzzled his stubbled cheek against the sensitive inner flesh. She gasped at the sensation, at his breath against her sex. He peeled her open, rubbing gently with his thumbs before he leaned in and licked her.

"Oh," she gasped, digging her fingers back into his thick hair.

He chuckled against her but didn't remove his mouth. He continued to lick gently, exploring, taking his time, finding all the spots that brought her pleasure and moaning when she twisted or gasped beneath him. He knew her body so well, learned by careful attention every other time he'd made her come, and he played her like a beautiful instrument, drawing her up to the edge of pleasure, keeping her there as she writhed.

Her breath came shorter and shorter, her legs trembled as the sensation mounted, as he added a finger to her sheath and she gripped it as she ground against him.

"Please," she whispered, not caring that she was begging.

He sucked more firmly, increased the gentle thrust of his finger. And she came, flying from the edge, her back bending, her fingers clenching against his scalp. He drew her further and further, never relenting as she moaned and cried out his name in the quiet. Only when she flopped back, the waves of pleasure becoming electric jolts, did he lift his head from between her legs.

She moaned again, because the vision of him, chin wet with her release, eyes bright with desire, was almost too much to bear. Had he ever been more beautiful?

"Enough?" he whispered.

She shook her head, shocked by the idea that he would give her this and never demand more. But she wanted more. "More. All of it."

He crawled up the length of her body and settled between her thighs, taking her mouth, letting her taste her own release. The kiss was slow and gentle, a tasting, a connection rather than a claiming. She sank into it and into him, reveling in his warmth and yes, his safety.

Would she ever have imagined that this overwhelming man could be her safe place?

No, she wouldn't think of that. She focused back on his taste and the way he was shifting his hand between her legs, rubbing the head of his cock across her wet entrance. She lifted against him and took him an inch. He broke the kiss with a shuddering cry and rested his head on her shoulder. He took more, farther, slowly, gently. Like he was reveling in her. She flexed around him and he grunted, his gaze flitted to hers.

"You know me too well," he whispered.

She nodded. She did know him, or at least his pleasure, just as he knew hers. He began to roll his hips against her, still so gentle, so slow. He bent his head and kissed her deeply, and she was lost once again in sensation. There was nothing but this, nothing but them, joined like this. Nothing but pleasure building between them, powerful and beautiful.

They rode the waves together, rising and falling as one, building toward release. She clung to his shoulders, loving how he trembled as they built higher and higher, knowing that she moved him just as he moved her.

He ended the kiss at last, burying his head in her shoulder, increasing his pace just a little, rolling his hips even more precisely. And once again the dam broke and she was lost to this and to him. She gripped him, her legs tightening around his thighs, her body lifting beneath him.

He was gritting his teeth, trying to give her all the pleasure before he took his own, but she could feel the strain in every muscle in his body. At last he withdrew and came, the heat of him splashing on her skin, as he called out her name in a long, helpless wail.

She wrapped her arms around him, keeping him against her,

smoothing her hands along the lines of him to learn them. To keep this in her memory forever. This moment where she could convince herself that this was not just gentle, not just safe, but something more. Something she'd have to learn to lose soon.

CHAPTER 15

Theo cradled Etta against his chest, tangling his fingers through her dark hair and measuring every breath she took. What he was feeling was something he would have claimed impossible a week ago, a month ago, a year ago. But every moment he spent with this woman, the depth of the love he felt for her increased.

Or perhaps that was the wrong term for it. He'd discovered more about it, but realized with startling clarity that it had always been there. He'd fallen in love with her when they were hardly more than children, every time they'd seen each other and his heart raced. Every time she'd fished or ran with the other children and he'd sought her out amongst the crowd. He just hadn't recognized it. He'd been in love with her every time he saw her since and dismissed it. He'd rekindled and deepened his love for her when they'd been thrown back together by Callum and Valaria's relationship.

He would thank his best friend forever for that shove he hadn't realized he was getting.

Now he so desperately wanted to connect with her beyond the physical. He wanted to *try*. Had he ever in his empty life wanted to try before? He couldn't recall. So this was another gift she gave him, because this purpose made him feel stronger and more complete.

"Why are you looking at me that way?" she asked as she glanced up at him.

He laughed. "How did you know I was looking at you?"

"I can feel it," she said, and the smile she flashed was false. She slipped out of his arms and his bed and moved away from, creating distance, as always.

He frowned and watched her look around for her clothing. "I sent it away," he said. "The gown was torn and soiled, possibly beyond repair, though I'm sure my servants will do their best."

She pivoted back, gloriously naked and wide-eyed. "Then what will I wear today?"

He looked her up and down, taking in every lush curve with hunger and adoration in equal measure. "The most wicked part of me wants to know why you have to wear anything, but I suppose you have a valid question. And I have a simple answer."

She held up her hands. "Which is?"

"This morning I sent a request to your home for your maid to bring a gown for you today. She should be here by the time we eat this lovely breakfast my staff prepared."

She shifted with discomfort and then nodded slowly. "I suppose Molly has already guessed what I'm up to. And she's discreet."

"Good." He motioned to the food he'd long forgotten when he had the choice of eating her instead. She blushed as if thinking of the same thing, but then looked at the spread of food.

"I *am* hungry," she admitted. "But what will I wear while we eat?"

He got out of the bed and picked up the dressing gown he'd discarded earlier. "This will do."

She took it and hesitated a moment before she slipped it over her shoulders. It was worlds too big for her, of course, but she looked delectable in his clothing. Like she belonged to him. Or he belonged to her. What a dream that was.

"But what will *you* wear?" she asked.

He looked down at his naked body. "You don't like what you see?"

She swatted at his arm playfully. "I like it very much. You know that too well, you pompous arse."

He shrugged, loving to have the playfulness between them return. He basked it in briefly. "I have another dressing gown. Let me get it, if you insist on covering me up so you won't be distracted by how much you want me."

He pivoted toward his dressing room and heard her laughing at him as he went. When he returned a moment later, she was already seated at the small table in his room, pouring them each tea and munching on slices of apple as she did so. He caught his breath at the sight of her.

She belonged here with him. Their mornings should always be like this, easy and sensual and filled with laughter and sex. He took the place across from her just as she pushed his cup of tea over. Flavored just as he liked it, of course.

They made plates from the bounty his servants had prepared and then ate for a while in companionable silence. One he broke as he said, "May I take you out today?"

She stared at him, fork of eggs halfway to her lips. She slowly lowered it back to her plate. "Out?" she repeated as if she didn't understand the question when he knew full-well that she did.

"Yes, I assume you are aware of the concept."

She arched a brow and pursed her lips. "Vaguely, Your Grace. Out where?"

He pondered the question. "What about a museum?" he asked. "Oh wait, you are not a fan of museums, are you?"

Her eyes widened. "Who told you that?"

"Flora mentioned it, I think."

She pursed her lips but he could see the humor on her face. "Flora. Goodness, if you go to a museum with Flora, you have to be prepared to be marched like a soldier to every single exhibit before you are set free! I told her I wanted to take my time, perhaps only look at a few things, and she twisted it all around!"

He held up his hands. "Then a museum it is. And perhaps a trip to the bookstore after. And then back here. To do more of..." He motioned to the bed with his head.

Her cheeks brightened to a deep pink and she began to nervously trace the edge of her plate with her fingertip. "That sounds lovely, but..."

"But?" he repeated, praying he could ease her fears, whatever they were.

"Is it...wise?" she asked, lifting her gaze to his.

He held that stare for a beat, another, then leaned across the table, cupped her chin gently and kissed her. She seemed startled by the action, but she returned the kiss readily enough. When he pulled away, he said, "I don't care."

Her breath caught and he could see her deciding if she should just run now. Make an excuse, perhaps even end this. But then she nodded slowly. "Yes."

It was one word, but it altered his world like an explosion. He couldn't hold back his grin of pure exhilaration. He felt the spark of hope now, because if she didn't pull away from these kinds of connections, that meant there was a chance for them. A chance for a future.

And he was positively giddy with the possibility.

Bernadette's maid clucked her tongue as she fastened the last few buttons on her gown. It wasn't that Molly was judgmental —she never had been—but every time she saw a new bruise on Bernadette's body, she reacted.

"It isn't so bad," Bernadette tried to say weakly. "It could have been worse."

Molly shook her head as she motioned Bernadette to a chair and began to fix her hair. "I suppose," she agreed. "I can't believe such a terrible thing nearly happened to you."

"There's a great deal I have a hard time believing lately," Bernadette murmured, looking at herself in the mirror as Molly twisted and braided and piled her hair artfully.

Her thoughts moved to Theo. The change in him that she'd sensed last night hadn't faded. From the way he touched her to the care he took with every detail of this day so far, he was changed. And she so desperately wanted to lean into it all.

Lean into him.

"It's a fine room."

Bernadette jolted and put her focus back on Molly. "Y-yes," she said softly.

"The duchess's chamber," the maid said, briefly lifting her gaze to Bernadette's in the mirror.

Now heat flooded her cheeks and she let her gaze move around the room. This *was* the duchess's chamber, attached to Theo's room through a small hallway. Since there was no duchess, the furniture was covered in white sheets, save for the chair she was sitting in and the mirror they were using to ready her.

Still, it was an exceptional chamber. The walls were painted a pretty pale blue, the window looked out over the garden, with a perfect view of a cluster of rose bushes that would bloom once winter was over.

She wouldn't see them, of course. Not from this vantage point. Whatever increased connection she felt between herself and Theo was born out of his fear for her accident. It would fade and they would end the affair as planned. He would go back to being her friend, perhaps a better one than before.

She would find a way to look back on this time they'd spent together with pleasure rather than sadness or regret or wistful wishes that couldn't come true.

"Lightmorrow is kind enough to allow me to use it," she said, arching a brow in challenge to her maid.

Molly was wise enough to return her attention to her work, but Bernadette wasn't under any illusion that the servants of both their houses weren't talking about the time she'd spent with Theo. When she hadn't come home last night and Molly had been called here to attend her, there had to be more than a few raised brows.

Not so long ago she'd been worried about that. Now it was harder to care because she had no intention of giving Theo up. Not yet. Consequences be damned, it seemed.

So she fought to remain calm and unaffected by anything around her. Something that flew out the window when the door to the chamber opened and Theo stepped in.

"Good morning, Molly," he said with a nod for her maid.

Molly seemed surprised that he knew her name, and Bernadette couldn't blame her. Why did he? She'd used it in front of him, of course, but no man she'd ever known, even her husband, cared enough to remember her servants.

"Are you almost ready, Etta?" he asked.

Her cheeks grew hotter at his use of their familiar nickname in front of her servant, but she nodded regardless. "Yes, we're just finishing up."

"You look lovely," he said softly, and the way his gaze flowed over her in a slow perusal made every nerve in her body fire like he was touching her. "I'll have my carriage readied."

He backed from the room with a slight nod. She drew in a sharp breath when he was gone but managed to finish her readying and came downstairs. Kimball was waiting for her. The older butler smiled gently as she reached him.

"The carriage is ready, Your Grace," he said. "And the duke has asked that you wait for him in the vehicle. He will be out momentarily."

She wrinkled her brow but didn't argue. She stepped into the cool air, bundling her wrap a bit tighter around her as one of Theo's footmen helped her into the carriage. She shivered as she looked at the place where she'd sat last night, remembering the way Theo had all but collapsed into her.

In a moment, he bounded in across from her with a wide smile, shut the door and tapped on the wall for them to move.

"You look very pleased with yourself," she said, not adding that he also looked incredibly handsome. It was very unfair how good-looking he was with his perfectly fitted clothing, his thick, slightly tousled hair and his bright blue eyes.

"I am," he said. "I have arranged for Flora and Roarke to join us tonight for supper."

She drew back slightly. "You did?"

"Yes, I knew they'd want to see you after last night's fright. And that you'd want to see them. They'll join us at eight."

"At your home?" she asked.

He nodded. "Yes, I thought that best, since I assume we'll return here after our day out." He tilted his head. "Unless that isn't what you want, Etta?"

She swallowed. "I just want to be sure I understand our arrangement."

There was a moment when she thought she saw a touch of frustration cross his face, but it was gone instantly, leaving her to wonder if she had imagined it after all.

"I'm not thinking of the arrangement," he said softly. "I'm thinking of my friend Bernadette and what she might need."

She let herself smile a little. "You're going to ruin your reputation as a rake if you keep this up."

He laughed. "I know, I'm on thin ice. All this rushing in and sweeping ladies out of harm's way, thinking of others, running around to museums instead of spending an afternoon analyzing every flavor of your skin."

She shivered at that idea. "You know, though, I'm starting to suspect you were never so much a rake as you pretended."

"Hmmm." He seemed to ponder that a moment. "I cannot say I was always well-behaved. Acting out, being seen as wild—they were ways to thwart my father when I had no other outlet to do so." His expression twisted for a moment and he darted his gaze away.

She nodded. "It must have driven him mad."

"I don't know." Theo shook his head. "He never gave me much reaction to anything, to be honest."

"That must have bothered you." She leaned forward and put her hands on his. He stared at their intertwined fingers a moment.

"I…" He let out a shaky breath. "I would tell anyone else but you that I didn't care about him. That he was a crusty old bastard and couldn't do a thing to hurt me. But with you, with you I must be honest, mustn't I?"

She'd been telling herself how dangerous it was to share herself with this man, and yet the idea that he might do the same with her didn't feel fraught. She wanted to know more about him. Wanted to take his secrets and keep them safe, keep him safe.

"You can always be honest with me, Theo," she said softly. "We're old friends, after all."

His nostrils flared ever so slightly. "Yes. We are that. The honest answer to your question is that from the day I was born to the day he died, I wanted his approval. I hated myself for it. I sometimes still hate myself for it."

"Why?" she asked, tightening her hands against his. "It's natural to want the love and attention of our parents. It's natural to look to them for acceptance. I know what it's like not to find it."

He frowned. "Yes. Do you see the earl and countess much?"

She flinched. She had never discussed her parents with Theo. "Only if it's unavoidable at parties. And when they demand an audience every month either at my home or their own."

He reached across and touched her hand. "What are those visits like?"

"Brief. Cold." She sighed. "They want to marry me off again. My father sees my availability as something he can leverage, just as he did the first time."

Theo's lips parted. "Is he pressing that case?"

"He hasn't much authority to do so," Bernadette said with a shrug. "Tunbridge was a great many things, but he left me well settled. I answer to no one now. My father can groan and demand and carp all he likes when he recalls that I exist. But he can't force me to wed again."

Theo nodded slowly. "Do you think...do you think you would ever wed again of your own volition?"

She drew back in surprise at the question. One she was not forced to answer because the carriage pulled to a stop in front of Montagu House. She smiled at the familiar lines of the big building. "Oh, this is my favorite museum in London."

He smiled as the door opened and he moved to go out first to help her down. "Shall we?"

He extended a hand to her and she stared at it. He was only asking her about going into the building, but somehow the question felt like it bore the weight of the world. Or at least of whatever their relationship was or could be.

So she didn't answer, because she found herself incapable of it, and merely took his hand so they could begin their day. She could only hope that looking at art and manuscripts and all the magic contained within those walls would clear her head a little.

Before she got confused over what was, what could be and what was just fantasy.

~

If Theo had gone into the museum in love with Etta, following her around the space had only made him feel those feelings more. Just like at the play the night before, he was enchanted by her utter focus on the art and sculptures contained within these walls. It was clear she was no casual patron, for she could give all kinds of details about many of the pieces and did so with a rapt, thrilled expression.

He could have followed her like a puppy through the halls

forever. Currently she was standing in front of one of the newest exhibits of sculpture from the Parthenon in Greece.

"Look at the detail on the horse's face," she breathed. "Isn't it magnificent?"

"What do you think of the recent report about the removal of the items from their homeland?" he asked. "The controversy."

She frowned. "As much as I like to look at the pieces, it seems wrong, no matter how much the report claimed it was done correctly. I'd rather see these things stay in their natural environments."

"Would you wish to go to Greece?" he asked, his mind dancing with visions of her floating through those ancient places at his side, discovering new history to be lost in. Eating amazing cuisine together. Making love to her as the soft sounds of the Mediterranean floating in through gauzy curtains on a hot night.

"Oh, it would be a great privilege to do so. But truly, I wish to go *anywhere*," she admitted. "It's one thing to live alone, and quite another to go travel alone as a lady. I fear I must content myself with books."

"Hmmm," he said, drawing his watch from his pocket. "Speaking of books, I think it might be time to go to our next stop."

She tilted her head. "A bookshop?"

He nodded. "I know you adore reading and I was able to make a special arrangement with Mattigan's for a surprise."

"Mattigan's?" she burst out with a little clap of her hands. "Oh, it's my favorite shop in the world."

Once again, he was stopped in his tracks by her enthusiasm. When she was comfortable with a person, when she felt free to show her true self, she really was a revelation. The idea that her husband had never bothered to enjoy these wonderful aspects of her personality was…astounding.

And hurtful enough that he couldn't help but recall she hadn't answered his question in the carriage about marrying again.

"Shall we go?" he suggested, offering her his arm.

She took it, still pointing out different facets of sculptures all the way to the carriage. Her enthusiastic commentary continued until the carriage door shut and then she suddenly ceased talking and shook her head with a blush. "I-I'm sorry."

He wrinkled his brow. "Why?"

"I'm sure I'm irritating you," she explained. "I can see your expression and I realized I've talked your ear off for so long. Sometimes I get carried away with subjects I enjoy."

He caught her hand and slowly shifted to her side of the carriage. Her breath hitched as he tilted her face up toward his. "I assure you, whatever look you saw on my face it was anything but irritation. I like listening to you talk, Etta. Passion is always welcome in my mind, whether that is in my bed or in a lecture hall or within the pages of a book."

Her expression softened, almost as if she didn't truly believe it, then she leaned up and kissed him. He wrapped his arms around her, returning the kiss with a fervor he realized was not perhaps the best idea when they had so short a time to get to the bookshop. But though it had only been a few hours since they last kissed, right now it felt like a lifetime and he wasn't about to refuse her if she offered him a taste of heaven.

She tilted her head, deepening the kiss as her hands clenched against his forearms through his thick jacket. He could be lost in her. Never be found. It would be perfect.

But at last she let out a shuddering sigh and pulled back. "You make this too easy."

"Too easy?" he repeated, refusing to release her even if they weren't going to kiss anymore. She felt too damned good.

"When I'm with you, I lose track of everything," she admitted, picking absently at a loose thread on his jacket sleeve.

"I like that," he said. "I like to sweep you away like that. Isn't that the way this is supposed to be?"

"I don't even know anymore," she whispered.

The carriage began to slow and he dropped another kiss to her lips before he reluctantly shifted back to his side of the vehicle. Though all he wanted to do was push this topic, he recognized that what he was doing by spending a day with her was at least sending a message that she was receiving: that being together was good whether it was in his bed or anywhere else.

He could only hope she'd be able to receive that message and not push it away.

CHAPTER 16

It had been an almost perfect day. If Bernadette had written out her every desire, Theo had met almost every challenge she would have presented to him. And he had done it without being told or prodded, with a soft smile and enthusiastic participation.

And yet she felt...not exactly satisfied. Even as she strolled through the shelves at Mattigan's, where she was normally perfectly content, she found herself distracted and out of sorts.

She and Theo had spent a little time after their arrival walking the shelves together, comparing which books they had each read. She had so long seen him as simply a playful rake that she found herself shocked by how much poetry he devoured and books he had read. He could easily quote lines from Walter Scott, Byron and Shakespeare. Usually so could she, but he flustered her.

She'd almost been relieved when he'd declared he had something to discuss with the shop's owner, Mr. Mattigan, and left her to wander the aisles on her own. And yet she couldn't focus, couldn't settle. Theo was on her mind. She strained to hear his voice, even though he and the shopkeep were talking softly in the distance.

"You are hopeless," she muttered to herself, and drew the first book near her hand off the shelf to force herself to look at it.

But she had not yet read a line when she heard someone say her name from the other end of the aisle. She froze, for the voice was as familiar as he own, despite how little she heard it anymore. She steeled herself and tuned toward it.

"Father," she breathed, watching as the Earl of Etheridge came down the aisle toward her, dark brown eyes so much like her own moving over her, followed by an expression of disdain. She fought not to buckle beneath it. This man was the first one who had ever made her feel unwanted, invisible. He'd set the standards for everyone who came after.

Except Theo, of course. Thoughts of him buoyed her up and she straightened her spine.

"Gracious, what a thing to run into you here," she said. "I thought you and Mama were in the country at your estate."

Etheridge shook his head. "Not this year," he said, and gave no further explanation of why they had changed their usual plans. She didn't ask. He wouldn't think to include her, as he didn't really think of her as part of his family anymore. Not unless she ended up having use for him.

"Are you a frequent patron of Mattigan's?" she asked, and frowned that she had to ask her own father a question very like what she'd ask a stranger because she knew him so little. Had he been a great reader? She couldn't recall.

"No," he said with another disgusted look. "Never liked book-shops. Your mother has decided to join some silly little book club and she asked me to pick up a copy of this month's selection for her."

Bernadette was surprised he would do so, as her mother and father were little closer than she, herself, was to them. "Well, that is…kind."

His lips pinched. "I am surprised to see *you* out at all. We heard about your near-fatal accident at the theatre last night."

Bernadette froze. Some part of her had known the story would circulate—there were too many eyes there for it not to spread. But for the news to have traveled to her parents so quickly when they didn't exactly ask after her regularly…it surprised her nonetheless. What didn't surprise her was how coolly statement was said. How little he seemed to care. Not surprised, but it still stung to be so dismissed and uncared for.

"Lord Etheridge." She squeezed her eyes shut as Theo approached and her father's gaze slid to him and then back to her with further disgust. Oh, this was about to get worse. Her father had always *despised* Theo. He'd always complained about him when he came up as a topic of conversation and went on and on about what a disappointment Theo had been to his father.

"Lightmorrow," the earl said, his tone icy. "I suppose I shouldn't be surprised to see you with my daughter. I heard you were her savior last night."

Theo waited a beat, and Bernadette realized that he must be waiting to be thanked for the service. Her cheeks burned, for her father clearly had no intention of doing so. She drew a sharp breath before she said, "He was, indeed. I'd been attending the play with some of our friends and would have surely been rundown in the street were it not for…for Lightmorrow." She found it difficult to call him by his title now.

"Indeed," her father said. "It was explained to me that he swept you into his arms like a hero in some children's fairytale and dragged you away from the oncoming beast." His voice remained steady and low as he held stares with Theo for a moment. "How utterly romantic."

Bernadette's heart was racing now. She didn't know why there was so much tension between Theo and her father, but it felt like it could be cut with a knife.

"*Brave* is a better word for it," she said before Theo could say anything. "

"Brave, yes." Etheridge shook his head. "And yet there are unsavory rumors going around about you and the duke. Likely from people who wish to add to the swelling story of the night."

"What kind of rumors, my lord?" Theo asked, his tone edged with concern and also...dislike. He didn't like her father, either, it seemed, though she wasn't as clear on the reasons. Not that the earl gave much *to* like.

"The person who reported the news to me said they saw a certain light in the duke's eyes as he looked at you after you were saved." Etheridge said. "But that couldn't be true, could it, Your Grace?"

Now Theo caught his breath and Bernadette swallowed hard. The undercurrents between her father and her lover were growing even more fraught. "Perhaps we shouldn't have this discussion in a public place," she whispered.

Her father didn't stop looking at Theo. "Where should we do it, Lightmorrow? In the parlor at your father's country estate? The same parlor where you were offered my daughter's hand fourteen years ago? The same place where you looked at me with utter disgust and told me...how did you put it...that you would rather *die* than be with her?"

Bernadette's ears began to ring as she pivoted toward Theo. His cheeks were red, his eyes wide as he stared at her. She wanted to find something in his expression that said what her father told her was a lie. But all she saw in Theo's blue eyes was that it was the truth.

And it felt like the world collapsed beneath her.

Theo had realized what the Earl of Etheridge meant to cruelly reveal in a moment before he said those horrible words. But he hadn't been able to stop him. And now he watched understanding dawn on Etta's face. He watched pain bloom there, betrayal. And it felt like he'd been ripped apart by a past he'd never wanted her to hear. Or at least not in this way.

He pivoted to her father. "What is the purpose of telling her that?

Is it to hurt her? Your only daughter? A woman who deserves nothing but good things?"

"Actually, it was to hurt *you*," her father said calmly. "You humiliated me all those years ago and I have not forgotten it. Nor would I *ever* approve of a union between you two now."

Etta's nostrils flared slightly as her teary gaze moved back to her father. "He hasn't asked. And neither would I. Perhaps I do not know much, obviously I-I didn't. But the fact that you would choose to reveal this so publicly and so cruelly...to use me as a pawn to attack a man who 'wronged' you over a decade ago...it tells me everything I need to know." She hesitated, her breath ragged before she said, "Do not reach out to me again."

Despite Theo's deep pain at how the past had cut her, when he looked at her in that moment, chin lifted even if it wobbled, certainty in her eyes, he had never loved her more. He had never been more proud of her for finally drawing a line in the sand between herself and those who would not value her.

"You can't talk to me that way," her father sputtered.

She shrugged. "I won't talk to you at all. That should fix it." She glanced at Theo briefly before her gaze darted away. "I would like to go now."

She pivoted and swept past him toward the shop door. Mr. Mattigan, who apparently hadn't heard anything of their quiet, destructive conversation, called out a farewell and she gave a weak reply before she exited into the chilly afternoon air.

Once she was gone, Theo stepped closer to her father. "That was poorly done, my lord. Perhaps you are too foolish to regret it, but you have lost something worth more than any fortune you have ever collected."

The earl glanced toward the door, uncertainty in his gaze. At least he considered his daughter a tiny bit in that moment. But then he shrugged. "As long as you won't have her, I suppose that will be enough."

Theo cringed at this man's cruelty. It was as sharp and cold as his own father's, the violence of it less obvious, but still a pointed end of an ugly stick. "If you come near her, if you bother her, if you say anything negative against her, I will find out," he said softly. "And perhaps you look at me and still see that eighteen-year-old foolish child who walked away from the one person who might have made his life…" He trailed off. No, he wouldn't say something so intimate to this man. "But I assure you that I have a great deal more power than I did then. I have a great deal more power than you have on your best day. I'll use it to make you sorry. So *leave her alone.*"

He didn't wait for an answer. He just turned and left, his heart throbbing as he saw his carriage in the street, the door open, Etta waiting for him inside. He could only hope that she would be open to hearing him out after receiving such terrible news about how he'd behaved in the past. If she wasn't, he might lose everything that mattered to him.

Bernadette didn't want to cry. She was fighting it with every part of her body and soul when Theo ducked into the carriage and it began to move. But when she looked at him across the way, his expression stricken and guilty, she felt a tear break free and slide down her cheek.

"Bollocks," she gasped, and wiped it away.

He flinched at her reaction and drew a shaky breath. "Do you want to talk about what just happened?" he asked, his tone neutral, carefully so, she thought.

"What is there to discuss?" She turned away. "My father behaved in a perfectly predictable manner. What was surprising was that I finally stood up for myself."

He nodded. "You were so brave, Etta. I was so proud of you." He leaned a little closer. "There will be a great deal of talking about that to come, I know. You'll need to feel things about it. To let yourself grieve what you've lost. But when I asked if you wanted to talk about what happened, I...I meant about what your father said about me. About all those years ago."

She turned her face. She couldn't look at him when she was about to ask him a question to which she already knew the answer. "Is it true?"

There was a pause that felt like a chasm between them. Then he whispered, "Yes."

"Then there is even less to talk about," she asked, and hated that her voice broke. "We've never made promises to each other. I never thought you cared about me or wanted a future."

He shook his head and there was panic that crossed his handsome face. "No. *That* isn't true. I have bungled this from beginning to end, I know, but Etta, the one thing I know for certain, the thing I wanted to tell you last night and this morning and all day was that I—"

She could see what he would say. He would tell her he loved her, perhaps because of the fright last night, perhaps to try to soothe her battered self-worth after what her father had so cruelly done. Theo would mean it kindly and it would cut her to the bone.

She lifted a hand. "Please don't, Theo. Don't do that. Don't say something that will only lead to more ruin in the future."

His expression collapsed a little and he bent his head. He looked like he was trying to regain his composure as he took a few long breaths. At last he looked at her. "I haven't earned the right to say that to you. I know. Especially after today. Nor have I earned the right to explain myself about what you father said to you. But what was said...what was done all those years ago, it isn't what you think, Etta. And I hope you'll be able to hear that at some point."

She swallowed hard. He was being, as usual, so very kind to her. But he'd always been kind, even just a few hours after he'd apparently told her father that he'd rather die than marry her. So perhaps she couldn't trust that kindness. Or at least she couldn't be so foolish as to tie it to true feeling. It was possible she was as meaningless to this man as she had been to her first husband.

The idea that she could be meaningless to Theo made her chest ache.

He shifted slightly when she didn't speak and inclined his head. "I realize you may need time. I arranged for us to return to your home."

She recoiled a little. "Oh. Oh, I see. I must have misunderstood what our plans were." God, he didn't even want to take her to bed anymore.

"I thought after the encounter with your father, after everything you went through last night, you might like to have a little time to yourself. I very much still want you to come back to supper tonight, to join me and our friends. But I would understand if you...if you didn't want to see me."

She should have ended things then. Thanked him and refused his invitation and written him some letter that would cut off this thing between them once and for all. Now that she knew his feelings, that was best, she knew. But she couldn't. She was desperate. She hated herself for it, but she couldn't change it.

"I'll join you tonight," she said, hating how her cheeks flamed. "Whatever happens, I don't want to make things uncomfortable for our friends. Or for you."

His brow wrinkled and he looked pained at that response, but he didn't argue. They were slowing in the turn on to Kent's Row and he surprised her by reached into the inside pocket of his jacket to retrieve a plainly wrapped package, a small book by the look of it.

"I got you this. It was what I was talking to Mattigan about before your father intruded," he said. "Perhaps you'll have time to begin it before we see each other again."

"Thank you," she said softly, fingering the spine beneath the paper and wondering what title he might have picked for her. As the carriage stopped, he leaned in.

"I know you don't believe me. After today, perhaps you have no reason. But I will think of you while we are parted," he promised before he cupped her cheeks and gently kissed her.

She was so stunned by that declaration that she hardly had time to return the kiss before he pulled away, tapped on the door and allowed the servants to open it to help her out. He waved to her as she backed up onto the stair and watched as he pulled the door shut and left her to her devices.

As she should have wanted. And yet she felt empty now that it was true. Empty after what she'd learned. Empty at the thought that nothing between them had been real. Empty that she might have lost him.

She trudged into the foyer, saying as bright a *good day* to her servants as she could manage. Then she moved toward her chamber upstairs, unwrapping the book Theo had bought for her as she did.

Her breath caught when the paper fell away. *Emma*, by the same anonymous author who had written two of her other favorite books of the last few years, *Sense and Sensibility* and *Pride and Prejudice*. This new release had been very popular when it came out at the end of the previous year. It had been impossible to obtain.

And yet Theo *had* obtained it and given it to her. As if he knew her. Knew her likes. Her heart. Were those the actions of a man who would rather die than be with her? The actions of indifference?

She didn't even know anymore. She'd felt the cold chill of dismissal for so long that the warmth was hard to trust, especially with those awful words her father had said ringing in her ears.

She shivered as she set the book on her nightstand and then lay down on the bed to stare at the ceiling. It felt like everything had been turned upside down from the moment that racing horse had barely missed taking her life.

And she had no idea what to do next, how to feel or how in the world she was going to face Theo and keep her heart in check.

CHAPTER 17

Theo paced his study, wringing his tingling hands with every step. Perhaps under other circumstances, he could have controlled his emotions, but he'd been stewing for hours, since he departed Etta's home, and he felt like a bottle about to explode from the pressure.

What he wanted to do was explain himself. Lay himself bare. Demand she hear his love and his excuses. But that wasn't fair to her because she had asked him not to do so. She might not believe him right now if he did. Which left him rudderless, unable to solve the problem.

God, how he hated that. And hated her cruel father for creating doubt in her as a child and now in their relationship. And for what? Revenge over what he considered a slight that had happened more than a decade ago.

"Your Grace, Mr. Desmond is here," Kendall said.

Theo pivoted toward the door. He hadn't even heard Kendall knock and he saw the butler's concern as Theo tried to take in what had been said. "Oh, oh yes. Send him in."

He smoothed his jacket. Christ, he was going to have a hard time keeping his thoughts and feelings from Flora and Roarke. They were both too nosy and observant not to see what he was going through.

As if on cue, Roarke entered the study. "My apologies for being so early. I had a meeting with Gray Danvers on this side of town about my investments in his project, so I thought I'd come straight here. Flora should be coming soon after—I think she was going to pick up Bernadette on the way." His forehead wrinkled as he looked Theo up and down. "Christ, you look like shite."

"Thank you," Theo said with a glare. "Just what a man wants to hear."

Roarke watched him for a moment and then said, "I've kept silent because I assumed you'd talk to Callum about anything troubling you—you two have been friends an age, after all. But since he isn't here, I think I must intervene. I-I know that something is happening between you and Bernadette."

Theo pursed his lips. "Flora told you?"

"She doesn't have to. I know my wife too well. And I have eyes, friend. I can see what happens when you two are in a room together." He reached out and clapped a hand on Theo's forearm. "I am capable of staying out of it when everyone looks happy and glows and blushes. But *you* look utterly miserable, so perhaps I can offer an ear. Or perhaps even help you, considering the problems Flora and I came through, ourselves?"

For a moment Theo considered putting Roarke off. Bernadette didn't want people to know their secret. But then again, she'd told Flora the truth, he knew that. And didn't he deserve someone to help him put all this into perspective? He felt like he was going to explode without that.

"You won't say anything?" he asked softly.

"On my honor," Roarke said, then he frowned. "And if that isn't good enough considering my past background, on my love for my wife. Which you know is true."

"I would never doubt it. Christ, where to start." Theo paced away. "I've been...I suppose it could be called imprudent. After all, I started an affair with one of my oldest friends. I took her to my bed and promised myself that it wouldn't matter. But then it was…it's her. Of course it mattered."

Roarke drew back and his surprise was plain. "Oh. I thought it was a lark."

"It was. Only it never was." Theo rubbed a hand over his face. "I knew that she was timid about it. About allowing herself to want for more. Her first husband was an absolute blaggard. A hateful man who made her think she wasn't worthy of love or desire."

Roarke flinched. "I knew him a little, thanks to my terrible cousins. He *was* rotten."

Theo nodded. "I had no idea how bad. Now I can hardly think of him without wanting to spit on his grave." He drew a few breaths to calm himself. This subject was too tender, he was revealing too much. But he had cut this vein open now and he could do nothing but bleed.

"I assume that her relationship with him and whatever lack of faith he created has impacted your…your affair?" Roarke asked, gently maneuvering the conversation forward.

Theo was grateful for the push and nodded. "Yes. And beyond that, her father has done the same. Something…happened today." He didn't want to speak what out loud. Didn't want to explain himself to someone else, even a friend, before he could tell her the truth first. "Her father did something that deeply hurt her because he wanted to use her as a weapon against me. And now Etta…*Bernadette*…isn't in a place to give any future with me a chance."

"Do you truly want a future?" There was no judgment in Roarke's tone, no opinion under the words. It was just a question meant to make him think.

Theo hesitated, not because he didn't know but because this was further vulnerability, but at last he nodded. "I…do. I want *everything* with this woman. But she thinks what's happening with me is noth-ing. She keeps telling me it's nothing. She wants to make sure everyone around her knows it's *nothing*." He sighed. "We spent a day together, a *real* day, and it was wonderful. And yet these doubts were rekindled and I still can't be anything more to her. She won't even let me explain what I did!"

Roarke blanched. "That is familiar."

Theo glanced at him. "Yes. I suppose it is. You hurt Flora and yet you came through it. How? How did you do it?"

"I remembered that she couldn't trust me...*yet*." Roarke moved toward him. "Bernadette can't allow you to explain whatever it is you've done...*yet*. And can you blame her? She married a man who had no regard for her. She has lived a quiet life. And up until recently, you two were no more than friends and you were playing your way through London. Add to that whatever it was her father did or said today...how could she have faith in anyone if she can't have it in herself?"

Theo considered that statement. He had thought of it himself, of course, he was no fool, but hearing it out loud in another person's voice made it settle differently.

"I suppose a handful of nights of pleasure wouldn't change her view. It isn't fair to expect it." He shook his head. "But I'm trying so hard to give her what she might need to see what this could be. I walk a tightrope between trying to show her what is true and not pushing her too hard. I thought I could do it, I thought I was getting closer. I was ready to confess my feelings to her and ask her to try to be more together. And then...this."

"Perhaps it can't just be about her. Perhaps it has to be about revealing *you*. Not about your desire, not about what you want from her...but your own demons. Sharing the parts that sting because you trust her with them. And want her to understand how you became the man she sees you as now."

Bending his head, Theo stared at the floor near his boots. The idea of being vulnerable, even with her, was...difficult. He'd built an entire persona to keep himself from having to be just that. "I don't know if I can, or I do that it will even matter. If I fail, I will lose everything and it's…" He cut himself off with a shake of his head.

Roarke nodded. "I understand the fear. To be so close to the love of your life and not be able to reach her is impossible. And to know that she might truly walk away, especially because of something you did, is even worse. Give her the space to decide, as difficult as it may be. Remind her that you are there for her, ready when she is. Remain open and vulnerable so that she may feel safe to do the same when the time comes. And hope."

"If there is hope," Theo murmured.

"I see the way she looks at you," Roarke continued, his tone gentler now. "From the moment I became part of your group, I saw it."

Theo sighed. "And how does she look at me?"

"When you aren't looking? Like you're *everything*, Theo." Roarke touched his arm. "Don't give up."

There was a light knock on the study door and Kendall appeared. "Her Grace and Mrs. Desmond have arrived, gentlemen."

Roarke smiled and Theo was struck by how happy his friend looked. It matched how he felt inside, himself, when he thought of Bernadette being in his sphere. Even now, confused and frustrated by what lay ahead of him, guilty over what he'd done, he also felt giddy knowing he would see her in a moment. He hadn't been certain she would actually come even though she'd promised to do so.

"Why don't we join the ladies?" Roarke said, and Theo realized he'd just been standing there, agog over the idea of seeing Etta.

"Y-Yes," he stammered, and motioned toward the door for his friend to lead the way.

But Roarke didn't move, at least not immediately. "If there's love," he said, "there's a way."

Then Roarke turned and walked to the door, leaving Theo there, hoping his friend was right. Hoping he could find a way to make this work. Because by God, there was love. And he couldn't let her go without making sure she knew it.

~

Bernadette had felt like she had been holding her breath the entire evening, waiting for one of her friends to say something pointed to her about Theo. Waiting for Theo to do something that would make whatever was between them plain. Or that he would move on her and try to make her ready to discuss things before she'd had enough time to find her breath.

And yet, as the night wound down...none of it had happened. It had simply been a pleasant night with good food and excellent company. Now she stood across the room from their small group, refreshing her madeira, and her breath caught. Despite everything that stood in the way, every fact that told her that nothing was real or lasting between her and Theo, for a brilliant moment she could picture this just being her...life. Oh, it already had been, of course. They had shared many of these kinds of nights either as a foursome or with all six of them gathered in one of their homes.

But what if she didn't leave him when the night was over? Not ever again? What if she could rest her hand on Theo's shoulder just as easily as Flora did now, standing beside Roarke as he sat by the fire, looking at the copy of *Emma* Theo had purchased for Bernadette?

She blinked the image away. She was a fool.

"I'm madly jealous!" Flora declared with a laugh. "I've been dying to read this."

"Well, I'll read it first," Bernadette said, wishing her voice didn't sound so hollow. She had to bring herself back to the present and not some future that wouldn't ever happen. "And then I'll pass it to you."

"Oh yes," Flora said, and held out the book for her. "And then to

Valaria. Though she'll pout like nothing else when she realizes I got the first read after you."

"Well, she shouldn't have run off and abandoned us for a romantic time with her husband, should she?" Bernadette teased, causing Roarke to join in the laughter.

But not Theo. He was leaning on the mantel, untouched drink in his hand, watching the three of them silently. He only smiled at her quip, and she tilted her head as she looked at him, trying to read him and his mood. Impossible.

Or at least until he returned her gaze. Then his eyes softened, his posture relaxed. They held stares for a beat before she forced herself to look away and find her breath.

Flora smoothed Roarke's temple with her fingertips and he looked up at her. She let out a sigh. "It's getting late—I suppose we should return home."

He nodded. "Yes."

Flora glanced at her. "Bernadette, may we offer you a ride home?"

Bernadette started. When she had ridden over to Theo's in Roarke and Flora's carriage, she hadn't fully decided if she would stay. If she did, one of two things would happen: either they would talk about everything that hung between them, including the past that still stung her when she thought of her father's cruel declaration at the bookshop. Or...they would go to bed together. They'd both pretend it hadn't happened, at least for a little while. And it would feel so good and so heartbreaking all at once.

Theo stepped forward before she had to respond. "I will take Etta. She and I have something to discuss in regard to the exhibit we saw today."

Flora's eyebrows lifted and she glanced at Bernadette. She nodded so Flora would know that was fine with her. "Very well."

She crossed the room and linked her arm with Bernadette's as the group of them made their way to the foyer. While the carriage was being brought around, Flora looked at her. "Perhaps tomorrow or the next day, you and I could meet. Take a walk in the park near the Row. Talk about…" She nudged her head toward Theo.

Bernadette shook her head. "I'm surprised you managed to not ask about him today."

"I thought you deserved a break after nearly being run down." Flora leaned in and kissed her cheek. "Enjoy your night. I'll speak with you soon."

She joined her husband and the rest of the goodbyes were said. Bernadette and Theo stood at the door, watching their carriage roll away. He looked down at her once it was gone. "I would like to put my arm around you," he said.

Every fiber of her being wanted to acquiesce to that. To surrender to what he wanted. To make this right and believe whatever lie he told her to soften the fact that once he had said he'd rather die than marry her.

She stepped away. "Theo."

He nodded. "I understand. I won't push. I just wanted you to know that I felt that way."

They turned back into the house and the parlor they had abandoned for the goodbyes. He moved to the sideboard and freshened his drink. "Did she give you much bother about me?" he asked, his tone light now. As if his request hadn't been made and denied.

"I assume you mean Flora? She does want to talk about you," she admitted. "But she gave me a respite today for some reason. She said it was because I was nearly run down."

"You don't believe it?" He stepped toward her half a step and she felt his presence like he had gone farther. Put his arms around her.

"I don't know what to believe anymore," she whispered.

He understood the double meaning, of that she was certain. He set his untouched drink on the table behind him and for another charged moment, they just looked at each other.

"I'm sorry," he said in a voice that barely carried.

She frowned at the sadness in his tone. At the feeling of it in her heart. When they'd begun this, she'd wanted to be certain it wouldn't harm their friendship, but it felt exactly like that now. Her pain and her heart, his guilt and their past...it made everything heavy and overwrought.

Somehow...perhaps in that moment when the horse nearly killed her...they'd gone too far. Opened a door she now had to close. And the only way to do it was to...end this.

She nearly buckled beneath that realization. By the power of the loss it would create.

"Bernadette," he whispered.

She flinched at the use of her full name, which he so rarely did. Another indication of how far they'd gone, how much they'd past the boundaries of this affair. God, she didn't want this. She didn't want this fraught and dire energy between them. She didn't want him to look at her like he had so many important things to say. They would either confuse her or break her heart, and she wasn't ready for either of those options. Not when she knew that this was over. That it had to be over.

She just wasn't brave enough to tell him. Nor brave enough to let him go. Not until she felt the full weight of his desire one last time. Not until she had one more memory to cling to, keep her warm when he was gone and life was...colder.

"I don't want to talk about it," she whispered. She saw him buckle a little. Pain and guilt doubling in those bright eyes. She didn't want that, either. Legs shaking, she stepped forward and caught his hand, lifting it to her lips, kissing his knuckles. He sucked in a breath, his pupils dilating with desire that seemed to erase everything else. Good, that was what she could control. That was what was within the parameters of their agreement.

"What do you want to feel, Theo?"

CHAPTER 18

Theo stopped breathing as he stared at Etta. She'd asked him the same question he'd been asking her over and over again during their affair. The question that led him to touch her as she needed to be touched. That helped him crack her open when she would not allow him access in any other way but through her body.

He didn't know why she was asking it of him now, when so much else hung between them. When she had only erected walls since the unfortunate encounter with her father. The only reason he could give himself was the worst one: that she wanted to use pleasure as a barrier. The same way he had many times with many ladies.

Even with her at the beginning of this affair.

However, her question gave him the opportunity to do what Roarke had advised him of earlier in the night: to be vulnerable. Even though he loved her, was he capable of such a thing?

"Theo," she whispered, her dark eyes holding his.

He wanted to be capable for her. So he drew a shaky breath. "I cannot express to you how empty my life has been."

She tensed. "Please don't. Let this be about pleasure now."

He nodded. "I know. I know you're not ready for the other. I'm not asking you to be. You asked me what I wanted to feel. I want to feel what you always make me feel, whether I deserve it or not. I want to feel...seen."

His words moved her. He could see it in the way the light entered her eyes. Feel it in the way that her hand moved over his and she squeezed gently. But then the fear returned, the doubt, the desire to build walls between them.

She leaned up almost painfully slowly, her breath stirring his lips as she whispered, "I see you."

Her mouth covered his and he felt his breath exit his lungs on a ragged sigh. She took advantage, letting her soft tongue move past and tangle with his. For a long time they simply kissed, with her taking the lead, exploring the same way he had explored her over the past few days.

But there was no controlling the wildfire of heat that those kisses ignited, and the shift in her was obvious as she began to make little sounds of pleasure in the back of her throat. He wanted so much to lay her back on the settee and make those noises increase and echo all around him.

But he didn't. He gripped his hands against the settee cushions and allowed her to continue. Her hand drifted down his chest, fingers clenching against his stomach and then his hip and his thigh. She massaged him there, working against the heavy muscle, inching ever higher toward the cock that was waiting for her. All for her.

When she traced him with her palm, he lifted his hips out of instinct rather than choice. She smiled against his mouth and pulled away. "What did you say to me what feels like a lifetime ago? Moan for me, Theo."

Theo was not a man accustomed to having desires driven by another person. *He* was the driver. But that order, said in her sweet voice, nearly unmanned him and she hadn't even unfastened his fall front. He held her gaze, sank into the sensation of her stroking his length through the fabric.

And he moaned. He moaned her name, he moaned his pleasure

and her face lit up with power. "Oh yes, I like that," she whispered. "I can see why you want it."

"Etta," he said sharply, lifting against her again.

She shook her head. "No. You aren't going to force me. Though I suppose if you want to beg me, I'll listen to your pleas. I will do what I do in my time and you will feel...*seen*."

She accentuated that statement by sliding her hands beneath his jacket and pushing it from his shoulders. He shrugged out of it and pulled it away. Then she tugged his cravat knot and unwrapped the length of it with painful slowness.

"My God, I see you," she said, her voice cracking. She unbuttoned his shirt and leaned up to lick the little path of skin she had revealed. He dropped his head back on the settee, moaning again because he couldn't stop himself. This was what she did: she stripped him bare, and he loved it. Longed for it. Felt safe in giving it, even with the pain that had been caused earlier in the day. Even in the uncertainty.

She offered him heaven and for the first time in a great many years, he shoved aside all thoughts and arguments and just...took what she gave. Her mouth moved lower as she spread the shirt wide. She tasted and teased and at last tugged at his waistband.

He opened his eyes with a smile. "Need help?"

"Take it off," she responded, then gave her own deceptively innocent smile. "Please."

He had never taken a shirt off so quickly. He thought he heard the fabric rend a bit before he tossed it aside, but that was something for this valet to deal with later. She placed her palms on his bare skin and hissed with desire.

"How are you so beautiful?" she murmured as she pressed her lips to his collarbone. She glided her mouth lower and swirled her tongue around his nipple, just as he had done to her so many times.
"

"I ask myself that about you all the time," he murmured.

She darted her gaze up and he saw the heated flash of her doubt.

Then she dropped her eyes away. He sighed at the battle they would continue to have, but then dragged his hand into her hair, tangling his fingers in the locks and watching them fall from the style and around his chest.

She slid her mouth across to the opposite nipple, swirling and sucking there, too. She made a little sound of pleasure in her throat and started to ease even lower, tracing his abdominal muscles with her tongue even as she returned her hand to his cock through his trousers.

He felt painfully hard and powerfully sensitive and the slide of the fabric against him made him twist against her with a low grunt. She smiled up at him, just a little wicked, and he nearly lost control again. No one matter how many barriers she tried to place between them, he knew that no one else saw this version of her. He wanted to be the only one for the rest of her life.

She shifted her weight on the settee and slowly came to her knees on the floor in front of him, pushing between his legs. He looked down at her, fully clothed, staring up at him, fingers moving to unfasten his trousers. The most erotic thing he'd ever seen in all his days.

She lowered the fall front and too him fully in hand, stroking him from balls to head. "Fuck," he grunted, head flopping back again. "Etta."

She gave a husky little laugh and then he felt the heat of her breath stir not his lips this time, but his cock. His eyes flew open and he jerked his head up. "You don't have to—"

She didn't wait for him to finish. Her tongue darted out and traced the head of his cock. She was hesitant, and he could guess why. Her rotten, foolish husband hadn't even embraced her enough to bring out the desire in her like this. But she still did it, circling him again and then taking just a bit of him into her mouth.

"Fuck," he repeated, drowning in the sensation.

"Teach me how," she whispered, stroking him with her hand again.

He tried to find words, thoughts when she was smoothing the wetness from her mouth down his length so perfectly. "Well, you—" he began.

She shook her head. "Not tell me. Show me. Let me hear what you like, what you want, Theo. Let me feel it."

His legs started to shake at that idea, the pleasure of it was so strong. He nodded slowly. "Put me back in your mouth," he said softly. "And I will."

She did as he asked, watching him as she took him a little deeper. He groaned and she stroked over him with her mouth again. She moved, she adjusted, she took him as deep as she could and then stroked what she couldn't manage. She swirled her tongue and when he barked out a cry, she did it again and again and again.

He was lost to her, lost to what she did to him. He gave over to it, allowing the sensation to wash over him, take him away. She grew more confident when he moaned for her, when he lifted against her in building pleasure. And she started making her own sounds of pleasure, like touching him meant as much to her as it did to him.

He wanted to feel that pleasure. To merge it with his own until they were both shaking for each other. It took a great deal of effort, but he managed to open his eyes, look down at her between his legs, sucking him with abandon.

"Etta," he grunted, and she looked up at him. "I want you. I want you to ride me."

She lifted her head from him, letting his cock pop from her mouth softly. He caught her beneath the arms and pulled her up into his lap. Together they pushed her gown up around her stomach and he cupped her bare arse to position her over him. She shifted and she felt the wet heat as he slid home deep inside of her.

She cried out, her fingers gripping against his bare shoulders, nails lightly abrading the flesh there and sending increased sensation through him. He lifted against her and she gasped out his name, driving her fingers against his scalp before she began to ride him.

She ground down against him, thrust over him, moaned when he dug his fingers into her backside and rocked her harder and faster. She was already fluttering with pleasure, instant and hot and powerful. He wanted to make her quake with it, forget her name with it, let go so entirely that she flew.

He lifted into her and kissed her, and she gasped against his lips, rocking harder, gripping him with her body, her wetness increasing as she neared the edge. And then she fell with a scream, rolling her hips, gripping him in increasing waves and milking him until his vision blurred with pleasure.

He wanted to come in her, to feel his pleasure match hers. But that would force her hand in the middle of a crisis his own selfish past had created. He would never be selfish when it came to her again. So he let himself come to the very edge and then he lifted her, coming just as she was gone. She rested her head against his, still moaning as he churned beneath her.

At last the ricochet of pleasure seemed to subside in them both. Their breath began to slow, match in the quiet. She lifted her head up at last and looked down at him. He wanted her to smile. To tease. To play until they staggered to his bed. Even if he knew they'd still have more battles to wage, at least if she did that he'd know they were on the right track.

But she didn't smile. Her bottom lip trembled instead, her eyes misted with unshed tears. And he knew what she would say before she said it.

"Every moment of this with you was...magical," she began, ignoring him when he shook his head.

"No," he said. Almost moaned, but this time with no pleasure.

"Theo," she said. "Please. You can feel the change just as much as I can. We never said we wanted more. And I appreciate that you're trying to protect me out of some kind of guilt or friendship or—"

"None of those things," he said.

She pushed from his lap and straightened her skirt down over herself. It was like nothing had happened between them. Like she had erased the pleasure they just shared. The same way she wanted to erase the connection they'd made since making the agreement to become lovers.

"Please don't do this," he whispered, his heart breaking. He'd never felt such pain before.

Her breath caught and for a moment he thought she might bend to him. Surrender to the emotions he knew had become a part of their every moment together. But they frightened her too much. After everything her parents had done, her husband had done...he had done, she had no faith in feelings.

"I must," she whimpered at last. "Please don't make it harder, Theo."

He bent his head. Every instinct in him told him that he should catch her hand and demand to explain himself and tell her that he loved her until she could hear nothing else. But he thought of Roarke's reminder that this woman had been forced into every situation she'd encountered in her whole life. And if he wished to win her, it would have to be on her terms.

He would surrender this day. But he would not give up the war until he was nothing but dust.

"If ending things will help you," he said, his voice trembling, "then I won't stop you. I won't make you be or do anything you aren't ready for. But I'm here, Etta. Please know I'm here and I'm going to be here until you are ready."

That seemed to surprise her, but she didn't respond to it.

"Shall I drive you home?" he asked, trying to keep things calm and cool.

"No," she said, too quickly. "If you allow me the use of your carriage, I can make it home fine."

Once again, he felt a powerful desire to refuse her that. To tell her not to go without him. But he didn't. He got up and put himself back into place as best he could, then sighed and unlocked the door before he rang the bell. "I'll arrange for the carriage."

As he stepped out of the room, he felt his face fall and all the worst and heaviest emotions at the idea that he would lose her washed over him. But even as he rang for the carriage, he pushed the wave of anxiety and fear away. She would go and probably distance herself from him for a while.

But that didn't mean he couldn't continue to try to prove to her, through letters, through gifts, through gentle reminders, that he did want her. Until she was ready to hear it and him.

CHAPTER 19

Bernadette lay in her bed the next morning, staring at the ceiling, just as she had been doing since three that morning. Her mind wouldn't let her sleep—it kept bringing her back to images of Theo the night before. When she'd made love to him, truly savoring his body and all the ways she could give him pleasure, it had been magical.

And when she'd ended things, she had thought his pain was real. And perhaps it was, in some way. She knew he did truly feel guilty for what he'd said to her father all those years ago. He didn't want to hurt her, of that she was certain. And that made him reach for things he didn't want. Couldn't want.

In a few days, he would forget his promises to continue his pursuit until she let him explain himself to her. In a few weeks, he would forget the chase of her entirely. And perhaps in a few months, they could just pretend none of this had happened and sit at a supper table together without her feelings making her scream inside.

At least she hoped so.

She grabbed for a pillow and flopped it over her face just as there was a light knock on her chamber door. She pushed the pillow away. "What is it?"

Molly entered the room slowly. "I'm sorry to come in so early, Your Grace, but you have a visitor."

"At this hour?" she asked, sitting up, heart leaping because she some part of her hoped it *was* Theo come here to demand she see him. To tell her…what? What did she want him to tell her? She drew a breath to calm herself. "Who is it?"

"The Duchess of Blackvale," Molly said.

Bernadette flew from the bed at that unexpected news. "Valaria?" she gasped out. "She and the duke are not to be home for a few days now. Is she well?"

"She seems well," Molly said. "She just demanded to see you."

"Fetch me my dressing gown, won't you?" Bernadette said, motioning for the dressing room where it hung. When her maid left, she looked down at her shaking hands. She had no idea why Valaria would be here, but she hoped she'd be able to crush her own heartbreak down to support her friend.

Molly returned. "Shall I tell her you'll join her in a while?"

Bernadette slung the robe over her shoulders and tied the sash. "If she came all the way here so early in the day, she must have a good reason. And I doubt she'll want to wait and I'll drive myself mad even if she does. Ask her to join me here. And tell Waterstone that the duchess may be joining us for an early breakfast."

"Yes, Your Grace," Molly said with a quick curtsey before she left the room.

Bernadette paced the room as she waited, ringing her hands and glancing at the door. Valaria wasn't like Flora. Flora was gentle, Flora gave space. Valaria would be direct—she'd been through too much not to be. Normally, Bernadette liked both those things, but right now she feared the piercing stare she couldn't escape.

The door flew open and Valaria entered like a storm. She crossed the room in a few long steps and tugged Bernadette to her. "I heard about your accident," she whispered against her shoulder.

Bernadette held her closer as she realized what had driven Valaria home so early. "Oh, dearest, I'm fine."

When she pulled away, Valaria's eyes were rimmed with tears. "I'm so glad. But I couldn't wait to see you. I told Callum we must race home."

"Oh no!" Bernadette said, taking Valaria's hand and leading her to the chairs before the fire. "How in the world did you even hear of this?"

"Callum took me to a little village not far outside London," Valaria explained. "To a cottage meant for two. And it was wonderful." Her face was lit up. "But we went into the village yesterday afternoon and were met with Lady Brentley. She immediately started talking about you almost being run down by a horse. She almost couldn't wait to tell me."

"Ugh, I'm sorry."

"I said I needed to go home and Callum immediately agreed. We packed up and rode through the night. We only just arrived an hour ago and I came straight here."

"I'm fine," Bernadette assured her. "I'm perfectly well. Thank God..." She trailed off, but then shook her head. No, she wouldn't pretend the facts away. "Thank God, Theo was there, he snatched me off the street and saved my life."

Valaria arched a brow. "Yes, there was a great deal of speculation about Theo and you thanks to the event in question. Before I left London, I ignored what was in front of my face out of respect for you, but I cannot now. What *is* going on with you and Theo?"

Bernadette hesitated. And there it was. The question she'd avoided, tried to pretend didn't exist to herself and others.

"I-I told Flora while you were gone." She ignored Valaria's gasp of outrage. "Oh, please, you were having a fine time."

Valaria smiled a little. "I was. What did you tell Flora, exactly?"

"Theo and I have been...engaged in an affair." That was true. "It's over now. I ended it last night."

She knew her voice wavered by the way her friend put her arm around her and squeezed. "Oh, dearest. I knew it. Although I had hopes it was more than an affair."

Bernadette got up and paced across the room. "I know you and Flora want to see love everywhere, the future everywhere, but I wish you could understand that I never believed that was my destiny. Especially not with Theo."

When she said it, she heard the lie of it. Of course she had wanted to see love in his eyes. Wanted to see the future. She loved him.

Oh, God. She loved him.

That truth hit her so hard that she caught the back of the nearest chair and clung there with both hands so she didn't fall. Valaria got up and moved to her, slowly, almost carefully, as if she were an injured animal.

"Bernadette, look at me." She did look up into her face and felt the tears begin to fall. Valaria wiped them away gently. "What happened?"

She told her, because she couldn't not. Told her about the affair, about the building hopes she had refused to name, about the fears that broke her down even before she heard the truth about the marriage arrangement he had refused. When she was finished, her body numb, Valaria stared at her evenly.

"What do you want to say?" Bernadette whispered. "To tell me I'm a fool for ever hoping?"

"I'd rather say you're a fool for abandoning hope," Valaria said gently. She drew Bernadette back to the settee and held her hands. "You have believed that you could not draw a man's attention or affection for as long as I have known you. Longer, if Flora is to believed. And I understand why, after all you endured from terrible men in your life."

"But..." Bernadette said.

"But Theo is not your father, nor your husband. You are right that he is a man who could have almost any woman he crooked his finger at. But he didn't choose any woman. He chose you. Not out of pity or duty or anything else but that he wanted you. And he could have also limited your interactions to his bed. He didn't."

"No," Bernadette admitted. "He didn't."

"But you won't believe he could care for you. Whatever happened in the past, you will take that over the present actions of a man who has been worshipping the ground you walk on for as long as I've known him."

"I—" Bernadette began, but she couldn't argue. Valaria was right.

"I look at you and I see me," Valaria said softly. "I thought the same thing you do. That the risk wouldn't be worth what I could lose. And it was a foolish notion that nearly cost me the love of my life, the man who adores me and protects me...the father of my child."

Bernadette stared as understanding dawned. "A child?"

Valaria nodded, her eyes brimming with happy tears. "I was almost certain before the wedding, but I'm absolutely sure now. I'm having a baby."

For the moment, all Bernadette's own tangled emotions melted away as she tugged Valaria into a tight hug. "Oh dearest, I'm so happy for you!" she said. "You will make such a wonderful mother."

"I hope so," Valaria said with a shaky laugh. Then she cupped Bernadette's cheeks. "But this dream would have remained buried if I hadn't risked something. Risked *everything* with Callum."

Bernadette sighed. "I know what you're saying, I do. I just don't know if I'm as brave as you are. Actually, that's not true, I know I'm not half as brave as you are."

Valaria smiled sadly and Bernadette could tell she was thinking of her terrible past. One Bernadette could hardly imagine. Then she said, "If you think you aren't brave enough, I will gladly lend you some of my bravery. But I don't think you need it."

Bernadette shook her head. "What do you suggest I do?"

"Let him tell you what he wanted to say yesterday after the encounter with your father. Let him explain himself. Don't decide what he feels without consulting him."

Bernadette flinched. "I would be no better than my father if I did that, I suppose."

"You will always be better than your father," Valaria assured her.

"And what if it doesn't work out? I won't be able to see him again."

"Then I won't invite him again. He and Callum can be friends at their club. I'm sure Flora would say the same."

"But *I* won't be his friend again," Bernadette clarified. "A friend I value."

Valaria bent her head. "I know. And perhaps hanging on to that friendship is worth more to you than having the future with him. Perhaps the risk isn't worth the reward. I'll support you either way, in any way, for the rest of our lives. But I truly hope you won't let fear of what you might lose keep you from embracing the beauty of what you might gain. I hope that nearly losing your life put that difference into perspective."

Bernadette stared at her. She hadn't allowed herself much deep introspection on what the accident meant. The fear had kept her from that. But now Valaria's words rang in her head. That moment when the horse had been bearing down on her, eyes wild and body flailing…what if Theo hadn't reached her? Would she have wanted him to know the feelings in her heart? Would she have wanted to leave this earth without allowing him to tell her whatever was in his, for better or for worse?

"I hate it when you're right," she whispered.

Valaria hugged her as response and sighed. "I know. I hated it when I was right for myself, too. So what will you do?"

"I'll go to him. Even though I made a very big scene out of ending things last night. I'll go back and I'll…I'll try."

"Then you'll already have done more than most in our acquaintance and I shall be endlessly proud of you. Valaria released her and smiled. "Would you like to have breakfast with me first? Despite my storming into your home and demanding you look at your life?"

"I want to have breakfast with you because you are the kind of friend who would do just that," Bernadette said with a laugh. "But only after you help me pick a dress to wear when I see him."

"That, I can do," Valaria said, and took her hand as they moved toward the dressing room where her gowns were hung. Where she would choose the armor she wore when she decided if she would declare her wildly beating heart to Theo and risk everything in the process.

CHAPTER 20

T heo strode into the foyer, shedding his coat and hat as he did so. The warmth of the house helped his frigid body, but a brisk walk in the park had not done what he'd hoped, which was clear his head. No, he was still spinning, uncertain, obsessed with thoughts of Bernadette. He had to come up with a game plan of how to approach her next. A letter, he thought, but he had no idea how to write anything without spilling out everything in his heart and potentially overwhelming her.

Kimball rushed to take his things, though he kept glancing down the hallway as he did so. Theo sighed. "What is it, Kimball? I can see you are barely containing yourself."

Kimball bent his head. "My apologies, Your Grace. The Duchess of Tunbridge is waiting for you in your study."

Theo had been holding his gloves in his hand and they slipped to the ground with a swish. "I-I must have heard that incorrectly. Did you say that Etta is here?"

"She is, Your Grace. She has been for about…" Kimball glanced at the clock in the hall. "Half an hour? She insisted on waiting for you in the study and I could not change her mind. I hope that is fine."

"It's...it's fine," Theo said, shaking his head. "Why would she come here unannounced? Why wouldn't she send word?"

Kimball blinked. "I...I don't know, sir."

Theo stared at him. He hadn't actually been asking the questions of the servant, more to himself, but he drew in a sharp breath. "What was her demeanor like?"

Kimball looked like a startled animal now. "I, er, she was kind, as always. Perhaps a little distracted. She refused tea. I'm sorry, Your Grace, I don't understand the question."

"My apologies," Theo said. "I am being unfair. I will join the duchess in my study. We aren't to be disturbed unless I ring."

"Of course." Kimball exited the foyer to take care of Theo's outer clothing and that left him to stare down the hallway toward his study. Why had she asked to be placed there? It was a place where he did his business—they had never met there. But perhaps that was why she'd chosen it. She didn't want to think about what they'd done in the parlor. Or his bedroom. Or once against the wall outside the bedroom when they couldn't wait.

But that still didn't explain why she was here at all when she had been so clear that she wished to end things between them.

His heart raced and he forced himself to move. "Only one way to find out."

He made it to the study in what had to be the fastest time in his thirty-one years of residence in this house, but once there he stood at the closed door, drawing in a long breath. He knew, down in his soul, down to his bones, that whatever happened tonight would change the course of his life.

And he hoped he wouldn't fail at it. Fail at her.

He opened the door. She was sitting at his desk. Not in the seat usually reserved for visitors, but in his actual chair, and he lost his breath yet again. She looked like she belonged here. She always did.

She pushed to her feet, a bright blush tinging her face tomato red, and swiftly staggered around toward him. "M-my apologies," she stammered. "I ought not have sat there."

He wrinkled his brow as he fully entered the room and closed the door behind him. "Not at all. You may make yourself at home in any room in my house, Etta. Always. Forever." He shook his head and gripped his hands behind his back so he wouldn't reach for her. "I didn't think I'd see you today. Or perhaps at all for a while."

"I know," she said with a shake of her head. "I made such a fuss out of leaving here last night. And I should have sent word. I should have left when you weren't in residence." She shifted. "Why weren't you home?"

He cleared his throat. "I walked to the park. I-I needed the brisk air to clear my head."

She nodded. "Yes. Did it work?"

"No." He laughed. "It didn't. God, I can't believe you're here. Do you want tea? Or bourbon?"

She glanced at the sideboard and he noticed there was already an empty glass there, set aside from the others. "I had a bourbon," she whispered.

They stared at each other for what felt like a lifetime and then he motioned to the chairs by the window. "Why don't we sit?"

She nodded, but when they took their places, she kept adjusting, moving, wringing her hands. Her nervousness was clear and his stomach twisted in knots.

She shifted and gripped her hands in her lap. "Did you...did you see Callum?"

He wrinkled his brow. "Callum?" he repeated. "Why would I see him? He and Valaria are to be out of town a few days more."

She drew in a short breath. "They came back today. I assumed he would come to you, close as you are."

"They came home early?" he asked. "Why?"

"Because of my accident." She pursed her lips. "Apparently they didn't actually travel far from London and word spread to them in the village where they were staying. I knew that this would cause a stir. She came to see me this morning," Etta continued, now absently worrying her sleeve. "And we talked about you. I wanted you to know that, to not keep it a secret."

"You talked about me," he repeated softly.

"About this..." She motioned between them with a shaking hand. "About everything that happened between us since they left London. I wasn't fair to you yesterday, Theo. I realized that when I talked to her."

"You were entirely fair," he said. "I know what happened with your father hurt you. And I know that you already doubted my intentions. You have a right to your feelings."

Her expression softened. "Yes. You are always willing to let me have them. It is remarkable."

Hope sparked in him at those words. At the look on her beautiful face. At the fact that she was here at all. Hope terrified him. "Did she tell you to come here?"

"Yes." She wrinkled her brow. "Well, no. Though I suppose she would have if I hadn't come to that conclusion myself."

More hope, and he tried to keep his expression neutral. "Then please, whatever you needed when you came, let me provide it."

She drew a ragged breath. "I realized, after some great consideration, that I had to come here and speak to you directly, rather than run circles around myself in my mind. Rather than deny you the opportunity to tell me the truth as you wished to yesterday. So please, Theo. Tell me about the night my father and yours tried to match us."

He drew a ragged breath of his own. "You don't know how much I hoped you would allow me to explain to you one day." He rubbed his hands along his thighs, trying to maintain purchase when his world was spinning. "I told you that my father was trying to push me. Trying to control me."

She nodded. "I remember."

"Before you and I had our talk in the gazebo, hours before, your father and mine met me in my father's study. They said they were going to arrange a marriage with you. And yes, I did tell them both that I'd rather die than marry you."

She flinched and he rushed to continue. "They were foolish words said by a foolish young man who pulsed with rage at his father. A boy who resented everything he had been denied when it came to affection or autonomy. I lashed out and said those horrible things that ultimately hurt you, but they were never about you, Etta. *Never* about you. They were about my father and wanting to cut him. To deny him as I had been denied."

She nodded slowly. "I can understand that. I can."

"But you aren't certain you believe me?" he pressed. When she was silent for too long, he couldn't take it any longer. "Then believe this: I love you, Etta."

As he had expected, that sentence changed her. Her eyes went wide and wild, her hands began to shake and she stared at him for what felt like a slow-motion lifetime.

"You knew I was going to say that to you before," he said gently. "It cannot be such a surprise."

"Knowing it and hearing it are two different things." Her voice broke a little.

"Then I'll say it again so it sinks in. I love you," he repeated, and God, but he felt free in finally letting those words out into the world, letting her hear them. Whatever happened next, whether he won her or failed, at least he would know he had been brave enough to risk his heart. "And I know I've bungled everything. All I can do is hope that you'll allow me a chance to fix it."

Bernadette was shaking, her mind racing as she tried to fathom what Theo was saying to her. Was it real, was she dreaming? She pinched herself lightly and the pain made her think it was real.

So she fought to reply to his statement. "You haven't bungled anything, Theo."

His nostrils flared and she realized he was *pained* in that moment. Those were regrets, from a man who usually was so breezy that it was impossible to think that he could have such feelings.

Only she knew him better, didn't she? She knew him down to his core. That was something she'd never wanted to pretend away.

"I *have* bungled it," he said. "Perhaps ruined it, though I hope not. And I did it not just when we started this affair, but a long time ago. I did it that night on my birthday when we stood in the gazebo together."

"Oh no!" she gasped. "Please Theo, I do understand that your harsh words that night were directed at your father and mine. You don't have to feel guilt for them."

"And yet I will. But that isn't what I meant. I meant after that, when I saw you later. When we talked privately. That was when I truly bungled things."

"I...I don't understand," she whispered.

"I had already loudly refused a match. But when we stood together, watching the sun set, I turned toward you and for a brief moment I thought of taking your hand and running away with you. On our terms. Making a life together that they had no control over and no part in. I thought for a blinding moment that I *should* marry you. Because you were the only person who had ever made me feel so...safe."

Theo, she mouthed, unable to actually form his name when her heart was beating so loudly and her hands were shaking with the power of that confession.

"But I walked away." His voice broke. "I told myself I was too young. I told myself I was overwrought. I told myself I would be happy in my emptiness. And then I tried to be so. Failed. When I think of the many things I should have done in my life, *that* is the action I wish I'd taken most," he said. He was quiet then, as if letting the words sink in, as if letting her come up with a response to this wild, unreal thing.

"Why?" she finally gasped, because it was the only word she could think of under this duress.

He tilted his head. "Because then I could have spent the last fourteen years knowing you and sharing with you. Laughing and crying with you. Loving you. I could have loved you freely all this time, instead of finally admitting it to myself in a flash when I almost lost you."

That brought up one final fear that had burned in her for days. She shook her head. "Then this all came about after the fright of my nearly dying?"

"My love for you?" he asked.

She nodded.

"No," he said firmly. "It did not. It was a powerful jolt to my system. But it isn't the reason why I feel how I feel. I love you, Etta, because you are so very kind, so very bright, so very beautiful. So perfect in every way that I more fear I do not deserve you than anything else."

He came toward her. She didn't have the strength to back away, to resist when he caught her hands, lifting them to his lips so he could kiss one and then the other.

"What I do know is that I *love* you with every fiber of my being, Bernadette. And I hope to give you every reason to love me back one day, if you'll risk pursuing a future where we are together, not as merely lovers, but as man and wife, duke and duchess, partners and friends."

She swallowed, and for a moment everything was so clear. He wasn't just talking about passion. He never had been. After all, they had both spent lives where they wanted more from those around them, but never received it.

That they could give that to each other could be the greatest gift either of them gave or received. If she were just brave enough to accept that this wonderful, frustrating, magnificent man could love her as he declared. To not compare her to the men who had been so lacking in her life, but to accept him for everything she knew him to be.

And she felt it so keenly in that moment that she could do nothing more than accept it. Because it was so clear on his handsome face.

What was even more clear was that he was just as uncertain as she was. His words had made it clear. "Did you say you *hoped* I could one day love you back?"

He flinched at the disbelief on her face and in her tone. "You don't think you could?"

She was silent a moment, then she slid her hands up his chest and cupped his cheeks gently. All the feelings she had denied, suppressed, refused to speak out loud for fear of turning them into weapons against her own skin bubbled to the surface, forced her to speak.

"I love you *now*, Theo. I love you and it terrifies me so much that I have been trying to make it go away for weeks, months, years perhaps. But definitely in the last few days that we've been together." She bent her head. "I-I love you."

He made a sound in his chest that she'd never heard. Something triumphant but also vulnerable, something filled with joy and also relief. He dragged her into his arms, hugging her close. She clung to him just as tightly, as joy replaced worry. As the future she'd been trying not to picture exploded like the king's fireworks across the world.

He leaned back. "You love me."

"I do," she admitted, and reached up to wipe a tear from his cheek. That her admission made him weep was shocking and moving. "I've been trying not to because I couldn't believe you'd feel the same way. And any evidence I saw to the contrary was just a fiction I was building for myself. But the thought of losing you, it has been killing me. I couldn't even last a day without running back to you."

"I'm so glad you did," he whispered, kissing her lips gently. "Because I never want to let you go. I want you to marry me."

She didn't hesitate them. Her joy was too powerful. She kissed him as she said yes, as she shouted yes, as she laughed when he picked her up and spun her around in a circle in his study.

When he set her down it was on the edge of his desk. His fingers dug into her hair and he kissed her again, but this time with more passion, more power. She lifted to him automatically, wanting what he would give, knowing it would be all the better now that they had declared their hearts and claimed their future.

His hands roved over her and hers over him as the kiss became more desperate and needy. "Later I'm going to savor you," he promised. "But right now…"

He pushed her legs open and she grabbed his hips, pulling him tighter against her. "Right now I want you just as much," she whispered.

He shoved her skirts up, she unfastened his trousers, they panted together as they shifted and moved to align themselves. He slid into her in one long thrust and then moaned, "God, I missed you."

She laughed despite the power of the moment. "Theo, you haven't seen me for all of twelve hours. And the last time you did, we were doing just this."

He began to thrust softly, grinding against her and setting her on fire. "I have missed you all my life, Etta. I've been lost without you all my life. And now you're home."

"Home forever," she promised as he claimed her harder and faster, as he pushed a hand between them to circle her clitoris, as she eventually shattered against him.

And while she was still clenching with release, he poured himself into her, his moan lost to her mouth, his body shaking against hers, claiming her body and soul.

EPILOGUE

Summer 1816

Bernadette couldn't stop smiling as she stood in the antechamber, arm locked through Flora's, waiting to be allowed in. They were both shaking and teary, just as she had been for the past twenty-four hours.

"You're going to frighten the midwife when the poor woman comes out," Theo called to her.

She pivoted back toward him and found him smiling at her, eyes just as bright with excitement and joy as she knew her own were. She squeezed Flora's arm and went back to him, letting Roarke join Flora in the vigil.

Theo opened his arms toward her and she stepped in, leaning up to kiss him. They had been married for six blissful months and she had never been so content, so absolutely happy. Every day she discovered something new about him, something remarkable. And every night he proved how much she was loved and desired and wanted at his side.

She turned toward the door as the midwife exited the room with a smile. "The duke and duchess will see you all."

It wasn't usual, of course, but the woman didn't seem fazed. That was likely why Valaria had chosen her for this, one of the greatest moments of her life.

They all entered the room quietly and Bernadette gripped Theo's hand tighter. Valaria was sat up in the big bed, Callum at her side. They both looked exhausted, but oh-so joyful. And in her arms was the tiniest, sweetest little bundle.

"Good evening, friends," Callum said softly.

"Come meet our girl," Valaria whispered.

"Oh, a girl," Bernadette cooed as she drifted from Theo and went with Flora to look at the red-faced, sleeping baby. "What did you name her?"

Callum cleared his throat. "Floretta,"

Bernadette straightened up and turned to look at Flora, who looked just as stunned as she did.

"As long as that is agreeable to you two," Valaria asked as she handed the baby up to Callum.

Bernadette took her friend's hand and Flora took the other. They were all crying now, joyful and filled with love for each other. Love she'd almost given up on.

"Oh yes, it's wonderful," Flora gulped.

Bernadette nodded in agreement. "For years we all suffered a lonely existence. And I think that coming to Kent's Row was a surrender of the future to all of us when we started there. But thanks to our time on there, we had met each other. Became best friends, sisters. And somehow we all also found love."

She looked at the three men who stood together, their friendship with each other as strong as hers was with Flora and Valaria. This was their family. Chosen and imperfect, but so beautiful. And it would only grow and blossom more in the years to come. She kissed Valaria's cheek before she returned to Theo and slipped her arms around his waist.

"Are you happy?" he asked, leaning in to kiss her ear. "Even though your time on the Row is over now?"

She nodded. "The Row was always about people. And with you, with them, with our life, how could I ever be anything but happy? Always." She kissed him. "Forever."

ALSO BY JESS MICHAELS

The Kent's Row Duchesses

No Dukes Allowed

Not Another Duke

Not the Duke You Marry

Theirs

Their Marchioness

Their Duchess

Their Countess

Their Bride (Coming January 2024)

Regency Royals

To Protect a Princess

Earl's Choice

Princes are Wild

To Kiss a King

The Queen's Man

The Three Mrs

The Unexpected Wife

The Defiant Wife

The Duke's Wife

The Duke's By-Blows

The Love of a Libertine

The Heart of a Hellion

The Matter of a Marquess

The Redemption of a Rogue

The 1797 Club

The Daring Duke

Her Favorite Duke

The Broken Duke

The Silent Duke

The Duke of Nothing

The Undercover Duke

The Duke of Hearts

The Duke Who Lied

The Duke of Desire

The Last Duke

The Scandal Sheet

The Return of Lady Jane

Stealing the Duke

Lady No Says Yes

My Fair Viscount

Guarding the Countess

The House of Pleasure

Seasons

An Affair in Winter

A Spring Deception

One Summer of Surrender

Adored in Autumn

The Wicked Woodleys

Forbidden

Deceived

Tempted

Ruined

Seduced

Fascinated

To see a complete listing of Jess Michaels' titles, please visit:

http://www.authorjessmichaels.com/books

ABOUT THE AUTHOR

USA Today Bestselling author Jess Michaels likes geeky stuff, Cherry Vanilla Coke Zero, anything coconut, cheese and her dog, Elton. She is lucky enough to be married to her favorite person in the world and lives in Oregon settled between the ocean and the mountains.

When she's not trying out new flavors of Greek yogurt or rewatching Bob's Burgers over and over and over (she's a Tina), she writes historical romances with smoking hot characters and emotional stories. She has written for numerous publishers and is now fully indie and loving every moment of it (well, almost every moment).

Jess loves to hear from fans! So please feel free to contact her at Jess@AuthorJessMichaels.com.

Jess Michaels offers a free book to members of her newsletter, so sign up on her website:
http://www.AuthorJessMichaels.com/

facebook.com/JessMichaelsBks
instagram.com/JessMichaelsBks
bookbub.com/authors/jess-michaels

Made in the USA
Middletown, DE
15 November 2023